Great Water, Big Sea

Esther Schultz

Backyard Studio Publishing

Harris, Minnesota

Published by Backyard Studio Publishing
Harris, Minnesota (United States of America)

Publisher's Note: This is a work of fiction. Names, characters, places, and incidents are a product of the author's imagination. Locales and public names are sometimes used for atmospheric purposes. Any resemblance to actual people, living or dead, or to businesses, companies, events, institutions, or locales is completely coincidental. Although some real-life iconic places are depicted in settings, all situations and people related to those places are fictional.

Book Editing and Formatting by JeanneFelfe.com using Book Layout © 2017 BookDesignTemplates.com

Publisher's Cataloging-in-Publication Data

Names: Schultz, Esther, 1978-.
Title: Great water, big sea / Esther Schultz.
Description: Harris, MN : Backyard Studio Publishing, 2022. | Summary: After marrying a man she hardly knows, Tuva travels with her new husband from Sweden to a new land, eventually settling along the north shore of Lake Superior in the Minnesota Territory.
Identifiers: LCCN 2022915632 | ISBN 9781737908630 (pbk.) | ISBN 9781737908623 (ebook)
Subjects: LCSH: Women immigrants -- Fiction. | Immigrants -- Minnesota -- Fiction. | Marriage -- Fiction. | Perseverance (Ethics) -- Fiction. | Minnesota -- Fiction. | Sweden -- Fiction. | BISAC: FICTION / Women. | FICTION / Historical / General. | FICTION / Family Life / Marriage & Divorce.
Classification: LCC PS3619.C48 G74 2022 (print) | PS3619.C48 (ebook) | DDC 813 S38—dc23
LC record available at https://lccn.loc.gov/2022915632

To my husband, Rod, who continues to be in this together with me in all aspects of life.

Chapter One

Sweden 1855

A string dangled off the lace, tickling Tuva's forehead as she glanced at her figure in the warped glass. Her mother, Elin Svensson, left the room, advising not to take too long. Tuva had told her mother she needed time to herself to make peace with her future before going down to the waiting carriage.

Tuva brushed at the front of her gown. The pale-yellow dress was the only one the store had, so she was thankful it was a perfect fit. It wasn't fancy, but it was brand new.

The lace donning her head was given to her by her grandmother before she died several years ago. It had been hers when she married, and she had wanted Tuva to have it. Tuva fiddled with the crown of myrtle leaves to ensure they were fastened securely over the lace.

Fear flashed in her eyes as she stared in the mirror. There was a small pounding in the back of her head. *I don't know him,* played on repeat, matching each throb of pain.

Her mother was all for the match. Her father was thankful he would have one less mouth to feed. Her little sister, Nora, just wanted Tuva to be happy. Thinking of Nora, Tuva made herself breathe in and out before forcing a smile.

"Tuva, come along. It's time to go to the church," her mother called from below.

Tuva's heart quickened and her shoulders slumped forward. She glanced out the window of her tiny bedroom and squinted at the trees in the distance. Bile rose in the back of her throat as she tried to bring the steeple of the church into focus.

"Please, Tuva, come on now."

Tuva swallowed. "Yes, Mamma, just coming."

She took one last glance in the mirror and straightened her shoulders.

"It will be fine. You can do this," she said to her reflection, and walked out of her room.

"You look just fine, Tuva," her father, Loui, said as she descended the stairs.

"Thanks, Pappa," she said, surprised at the rare compliment. She moved to hug her father, but he turned away. Tuva tried to push the rejection out of her thoughts but the sting in her heart would not fade.

Tuva followed her father out to the waiting carriage, where she was swept up to a seated position next to her sister. It only took a few minutes to arrive at the church, but with every clop of the horses' hooves, the pounding in her heart grew stronger. The carriage stopped at the front entrance and a small boy ran into the church to announce their arrival.

Inhaling, Tuva attempted to calm the nerves shuddering through her body, but her mother nudged her to leave the safe confines of the carriage.

"Come now, no cold feet. It will be good. You will see."

"I know, Mamma. I just—"

"You just what?" her mother asked. "Oh, never mind. Come on now."

"Yes. Okay," Tuva mumbled. She gathered her gown into her hands to walk the short distance to the front of the church and her waiting groom, careful not to get the hem dirty. Her family disappeared and she was left alone with him. Her apprehension kept her from looking in his direction. Instead, she focused on her every move. As soon as her gown was smoothed out, the church doors flew open, and the ceremony began.

Ready or not, I'm about to be married.

The service lasted about thirty minutes, and as the minister neared the end, Tuva was fidgeting. She shifted from one foot to the other, the coins in her shoes digging into the bottom of her feet, while her soon-to-be husband seemed calm.

I just might collapse.

Tuva flinched as her groom pulled her into their marriage kiss. From somewhere in the fog of her mind she heard, "Mr. and Mrs. Isak Nilsson are now wed."

While she walked with her groom toward the rear of the church, Tuva's head spun. She glanced up at her husband and realized he was gazing at her with such gentleness. He looked happy.

The tension eased out of her body at seeing Isak's pleasure.

Maybe this will be okay. Maybe.

With lighter spirits, Tuva dove into the excitement of the wedding reception at her parents' home. Food and drinks were served, and people mingled for hours.

Adam, Isak's brother, took out his fiddle and started to play a lively tune. Isak grabbed Tuva's hand and they started to dance. She whooped and hummed along with the tune until the song was over and Isak leaned down to kiss her.

Heat shot through her, and she gasped for air when Isak released her. He winked at her, clasped her hand, and led her back to their seats while stepping to the beat of the new song being played. Tuva giggled at his playfulness and any remaining fears melted away.

Once the latest song finished, Isak stood on top of his chair and hollered, "If I could have your attention." He paused, the crowd quieted, and he looked down at Tuva. "I'm a blessed man by marrying such a fine woman today. I look forward to our many years together, and if our love could grow into the same love my parents have, then I will be the happiest of men."

The crowd applauded, and Tuva could feel the heat in her cheeks rise at the attention. Isak paused, and the group quieted again. "I have, for my bride, the greatest of wedding presents. I was fearful that they would not arrive in time. But they have. As some know, my parents, along with my youngest brother, moved to America several years ago. Father has been working diligently to make it happen, and it finally has."

Isak took a sip of his beverage and Tuva thought she was going to throw up. With every word her husband said, she knew it was leading to only one thing, and the idea terrified her.

"We are moving to America," Isak shouted. "We set sail in two days' time."

The color drained from Tuva's cheeks. Her ears started ringing. She looked over at her parents and little sister and wondered what they were thinking.

Her father was smiling, her mother seemed confused, and her little sister had tears running down her cheeks. Tuva skimmed the crowd and realized the rest of the guests were celebrating.

People kept saying it was a gracious gift, and how wonderful it was, and they wish it was them. But Tuva couldn't fathom leaving the only home she had ever known. How could she leave her country to start a new life with a man and a family she didn't know?

Isak embraced her and whispered, "I can tell you're not as excited as I. I was hoping you would be, but I know in time you will grow to be just as happy."

Tuva forced her lips to curve upward, but she was crying inside. It seemed like Isak could read her every expression. He eased back, but instead of letting her go, he kept his arm around her as though he were offering her the strength she needed to get through the rest of the reception. Thankfully, it didn't last much longer. When the last of their friends left, Isak gathered Tuva's trunks and prepared his carriage to take her to his family home a short distance away.

Tuva rode in silence next to her new husband and wondered at what the next couple of hours would bring her. Her mother had given her some basic information of what to expect on her wedding night, but she really knew nothing. When the carriage stopped in front of the Nilsson farmhouse, thoughts of jumping and running back to her parents' home flitted through her mind.

Isak cradled her hand and said, "It will be okay, Mrs. Nilsson. I promise to take care of you."

Tuva's shoulders slumped and she squeezed Isak's hand. "Thank you for trying to reassure me. It's been a day of all kinds of emotions."

"I could tell this was a hard day for you," Isak said. "But I hope you know how much I care for you, Tuva, and I can't wait for us to grow together and learn to love one another properly."

"You are such a kind man, Isak."

He flashed a grin and hugged her to him. "I hope you always see kindness in me."

Tuva melted in her husband's arms just as he whisked her up and ran to the front door. His laughter was contagious, and she couldn't resist the giggles rising inside her. He flung the front door open and kissed her soundly.

When he finally let her go, Tuva's heart was pounding. Longing consumed her and she tried to make sense of it.

Isak motioned for her to sit in a rocking chair by the fireplace and kissed her on the cheek. "I will go grab your things."

The door shut behind him, and Tuva glanced around the room. It was a tiny home. Smaller than her own, but well maintained. She wondered what would happen to the little homestead once they left. She sat by the fireplace watching her husband make the few short trips carrying her trunks and grew restless.

She rummaged around the kitchen area to see what food was available. She found only a few eggs, half a loaf of bread, some cheese, and a few vegetables. Tuva grabbed a skillet and fried some eggs and vegetables. She cut a few slices of bread and cheese and set the table. She was just finishing her chore when Isak sidled up beside her.

"Smells good," he said.

"Thank you. It's really nothing. Just a few items thrown together with what I could find."

"Perhaps, but I'm glad you felt at home enough to make us a small meal," Isak said. "I haven't held on to a lot since discovering our papers came through for us to go, so I'm sorry there isn't more."

"I suppose that makes sense," she said, and tried to hide her face at the mention of sailing away from home.

"I know this is a shock for you. But I know we will have a great adventure."

"An adventure? Maybe," Tuva said, "but I'm the one leaving my family behind. You're at least going with your family."

Isak stepped closer and said, "Please don't cry. I wouldn't be able to bear it."

Tuva gulped back the tears threatening to spill over. "I'm trying not to, but I don't know how you expect me not to cry. In less than a day, I have married a man I don't really know. I have learned that I'm leaving my home forever, and I probably will never see my family again. My entire world is upside down."

Isak wrapped his arms around her. "Well then, go ahead and cry."

She let the dam break, allowing the emotions from the day to flow while Isak held her, saying nothing.

As she regained her composure, Isak wiped her cheeks and kissed her on the nose. "Feel better?"

Tuva shifted so she could look directly in to Isak's eyes. "I feel much better. Thank you for letting me cry."

"Anything for you, my Tuva."

Something new to Tuva passed between them, and she leaned in to kiss Isak. This was the first time she had made the first move, and it seemed to ignite something inside her husband. He gathered her closer, and she rode the wave of desire with him until he picked her up and carried her to the bed in the next room.

"What about dinner?" she asked as Isak gently laid her on the bed.

"It can wait."

Chapter Two

Tuva stood at the window in the kitchen, breathing in the nutty aroma pouring out of her hot mug. She took a sip of her coffee, enjoying the full-bodied flavor as she stared at the rising sun. She shivered at the memory of her night with her new husband and wanted to jump back into bed to pick up where they left off. She turned away from the window, her hopes dashed, as Isak emerged from the bedroom.

"You are just beautiful. I like your hair down with those soft curls framing your face." He reached to push one back. "And how delightful your blue eyes are, shining at me from behind that smug smile."

Tuva giggled at his description. "You look pretty smug yourself. Handsome. But smug."

It was Isak's turn to laugh while he filled his own cup of coffee. Tuva crossed the room to sit at the kitchen table and pulled the lid off the pan in the center. "I have eggs and vegetables and some bread and cheese for you."

"Food and coffee ready for me," Isak said. "You spoil me."

"Or you're just not used to having a woman around."

"Perhaps you're right."

Tuva dished their plates, and Isak winked at her before they started to eat. Tuva listened to forks scrapping against tin and tried not to feel awkward.

She fidgeted at the lack of conversation, so asked, "Can you tell me what it will be like?"

Isak paused, his fork halfway to his mouth. "What will it be like?"

"Yes, the passage over? Where are we going? Your parents? Are you able to share anything about our journey?"

Isak set his fork down. "Um, let's see. The passage will be on a large ship which holds hundreds of people. We will be sharing a room with my brother. I know the arrangements aren't the best for a newly married couple, but it was the cheapest way for all three of us to go, and it was all we could afford. We will arrive in New York City, and most likely spend some time there. Once we finalize details, we will take a train as far as it will go, and continue on boats and wagons until we arrive at a place called the Minnesota Territory."

"Minnesota Territory? I have never heard of it," Tuva said. "Is it nice?"

"Mamma's letters say the winters can be harsh, but that it's pretty. She says it reminds her of here."

"What will we do when we get there?"

"I suppose I will help Pappa with his farm, and you will help Mamma in the kitchen, the small garden, and whatever else she needs. That is, until we can manage to get our own place," Isak said.

"Okay. Well, that sounds nice."

"I'm sure it will be," he said. "I'm excited to go."

Tuva's muscles tightened and her stomach dropped as she continued to contemplate everything Isak had explained to her. She forced her bite down her throat. "Do you think your mother will like me?"

Isak looked surprised by the question. "I believe she will. She will be happy to have a daughter at last."

Tuva started to take another bite when there was a knock at the front door. She placed her fork back on her plate, while Isak crossed the room to answer it.

"Why are you knocking?" Isak asked the person at the door. He stepped back, and his younger brother walked in.

"I wanted to make sure you were up and around, before just barging in here," Adam said, ringing his hat in his hands. He looked sheepish as he turned toward Tuva. "Good morning, sister."

"Good morning." Tuva grinned and rose from her chair. "Can I fix you a plate?"

Adam's stomach growled and Tuva burst into laughter.

"That would be great," Adam said, chuckling with her as he wound his way to a seat at the table.

Fixing her new brother-in-law a plate, Tuva set it in front of Adam and went back to her own chair. They ate the small breakfast with comments about the weather and the day's chores.

They were just finishing when Tuva asked, "Would you mind terribly if I went and visited my family today? Especially since we are leaving tomorrow."

Isak leaned across the table, reaching for Tuva's hand. "You must visit them. And when you return, we will make final preparations for our trip."

"Thank you for understanding. I will clean the kitchen and head over."

Isak nodded and stood with his brother to start their own chores for the day.

Tuva skimmed her fingers over the pile of lace. It was lying on the kitchen table she had eaten at all her life. Her mother had made her a few lace curtains and table covers as a wedding present, but in the excitement of the previous day's events, had forgotten to give them to her. Tuva took another sip of her coffee, enjoying its bold flavor, and asked, "Are you okay with me leaving, Mamma?"

"Am I okay with it?" Her mother paused, took a deep breath, and said, "I will miss you terribly, but I know you will have a better life there."

"And what about Pappa and Nora?"

"Your Pappa isn't sentimental. Nora is sad," her mother said. "But you mustn't let that stop you. You are married now and must go where your husband goes."

"I know, but I can't imagine life without having you and Pappa and Nora with me," Tuva said. "And to be honest, I'm a little scared of what is to come. A strange land. A new family. I don't know what to expect."

"Expect nothing," Mamma said. "It's an adventure. You are getting to do something that no one in our family would have imagined we could ever do."

A rustling of feet caught Tuva's attention and she turned just as Nora bounded into the room with something behind her back.

"What do we have here, little sister?" Tuva asked.

"It's a gift. From me to you. I thought I would have longer," Nora paused, started again. "I thought I would have longer to finish it, but since I don't, I finished it last night. Pappa made the frame."

Nora thrust the package into Tuva's hands while Tuva fumbled with her mug. Black liquid sloshed over the rim before Tuva could set it down.

"Gracious, child, calm down. She isn't leaving in the next five minutes," Mamma said.

"Sorry, Tuva," Nora said. "I'm just excited for you to see it."

Tuva tore open the paper, and her hand flew to her mouth. "Oh!"

Nora had sketched a portrait of their parents, Nora, and her. Tuva stared into the eyes of her family before hugging the picture to her chest.

"Nora, it's beautiful." Tuva lowered the frame to her lap and skimmed her fingers over the glass covering the drawing.

"The final details are rushed," Nora said.

"It doesn't matter. It's just breathtaking. I will treasure it always," Tuva said as she dabbed at her damp cheeks.

Tuva hugged her sister, and Nora asked, "When do you leave?"

Leaning back in her chair, Tuva said, "We head out first thing tomorrow. We will be staying the night in Gothenburg, then boarding the following morning."

"Promise you will write," Nora said as she sat in the closest chair.

"Of course, I will write. I promise. I will do so as often as possible."

Tuva glanced at her mother and noticed moisture in the corner of her eyes. She stood, walked to her, and wrapped her arms around her.

They held each other and cried before her mother eased away, wiping her face with her apron. "Come now. We must be strong."

"We can be strong and sad at the same time, Mamma."

"When did you become so wise, Tuva."

"Apparently when I became a married woman," Tuva said with a chuckle.

Her mother and Nora joined her before Tuva changed the subject to Nora's plans and education, since she would be the oldest child at home now. Tuva stayed through lunch even though her father insisted she should be home with her husband. The women outnumbered him, and Tuva couldn't care less if he was angry at her for shirking her wifely duties. She wanted to spend as much time as possible with her sister and mother before having to say the dreaded goodbye.

Before Tuva had time to prepare, the sun started to lower in the sky, signaling she had to leave her family. Mother and daughters held each other and let the tears flow until Tuva had to pull away to start her trek home.

Before leaving, Tuva stopped in the barn to say her goodbyes to her father. He was gruff to her, but allowed her to hug him. When she started to pull away, he finally wrapped his arms around her and said, "Do us proud, my daughter."

"I love you, Pappa," Tuva said as she went to leave.

He stared at Tuva for an eternity before saying, "Me too, daughter." Turning away from her, he jumped back into his work.

It was the closest thing to I love you Tuva had ever received from him, and she would take it. She brushed away the tears and headed toward her waiting husband. They had a busy evening of final preparations ahead of them.

Chapter Three

Tuva stood on the dock staring up at the grand ship. She thought her knees would buckle as she started to sweat, realizing this beast would be taking them to her new country. She would have pinched herself if she wasn't standing in a crowd of people.

She was in line to board with Isak and Adam, and wondered at the accommodations they would have. She knew some passengers would have to ride in the belly of the ship, and she wasn't sure if she could handle those types of arrangements.

The wait passed quickly, and they were next to board. Tuva closed her eyes, took a deep breath. *Who am I to make such a trip?* Releasing the air out of her lungs, her spirits lifted. She opened her eyes and stepped onto the ship.

Tuva followed her husband through the corridors, thankful he seemed to know where to go. Adam trailed behind her with a few of their bags in tow. The rest of their trunks would be delivered by the ship's crew later that day.

Isak stopped before a door, took out his key, and unlocked it. When the door opened, Tuva was surprised at how cramped it was. She remembered they would all be sharing the same room, but was not expecting it to be so small.

A tiny seating area nestled against a double bed that buffeted the wall. A small washing stand was anchored next to the screen for changing. A window that cracked open to allow for fresh air washed away her disappointment in the space, and she decided to make the best of her situation.

It will have to be doable.

She set about putting a few items away and tried pushing thoughts of their journey out of her head.

"That was nice of your family to see us off when we started our journey to Gothenburg," Isak said as he stared out the window.

Tuva's brows furrowed as the memory of her mother and Nora waving flashed through her mind. She didn't want to be thinking about them, as it made her sad. She tidied the last of the items and walked over to Isak.

"What are you looking at?" she asked.

"My home country," Isak said. "I'm excited to see my family on the other side of the ocean. But I'm suddenly sad to leave our farm and Floda, knowing I probably won't ever return."

Hugging Isak, Tuva said, "I understand the feelings. The finality of what we are about to do is overwhelming even if one is excited like you are. Come, let's go on deck to get a better look and say a proper goodbye to our homeland."

"That's a great idea," Adam said from across the room.

Tuva jolted and her hand flew to her chest. "Adam, I forgot you were here. Traveling with both of you will take some getting used to, I think."

They made their way back through the corridors to the top deck along with other passengers, who apparently had the same idea. They found a good spot to look out, and Tuva watched the comings and goings of the people below. There were shouts from the crew signaling their departure, and Tuva felt a slight shudder as they cast off.

People below waved and shouted to those on the ship. The people on the ship cried out in return. Tuva gestured wildly at her country, tears streaming down her cheeks.

"Goodbye, my country. Goodbye, my home."

Chapter Four

The sway of the boat deepened, and Tuva glanced at the window. Her heart quickened at seeing darkness instead of light.

She placed her book on the table next to her, walked over to take a better look, and gasped. "Isak, where is Adam?"

Isak looked up from the paper he was writing on. "What is it?"

"The seas are getting rough, and dark clouds are forming. I'm a little worried that this may be as bad as the last storm, the one where we lost someone overboard."

"Surely it couldn't be that bad." Isak crossed the room to stand next to her. He peered outside before looking down at Tuva. She could tell he was fighting to hide his concern when he said, "I will go in search of Adam."

"And I will secure our things," Tuva said.

She walked around the room, gathering loose items. She snatched her book and secured it with the rest of their belongings. Tuva paused in front of the window whenever she walked by while she continued to prepare. She tried to keep her thoughts in check until Isak returned with Adam.

They were whispering as they entered the room, and Tuva said, "Don't keep it from me. Explain, please."

Isak and Adam exchanged concerned glances before Adam said, "The captain fears this is the worst storm yet."

"Why would you say that?" Isak asked.

"Because she has a right to know what we are facing," Adam said.

"Well, I don't want her to be frightened," Isak said.

"I'm sure she would rather we were honest," Adam said.

"Gentlemen," Tuva interrupted. "I'm standing right here. Please don't talk as though I'm not."

"Apologies, but I just want to keep you safe," Isak said.

"Keeping things from me or lying to me is not keeping me safe," Tuva said.

The boat dipped, and Tuva lost her footing, careening into Adam. Isak reached out to grab her, but fell into her instead. Adam slammed into the wall and Tuva could tell he was trying to steady all three of them before they fell to the floor.

Tuva yelped when she whacked her arm on the changing screen bolts, which anchored it to the floor.

Isak jumped up and tried to secure her, but another shift knocked him off his feet, and he rolled away from her. Adam slid to his hands and knees and crouched like he was bracing himself against the next wave.

"Isak, get on all fours and crawl toward the wall closest to the chairs. I will help Tuva since I'm beside her," Adam directed.

"I will help my wife!" Isak demanded, but as he made another attempt toward her, the boat pitched, and he fell backwards.

"I'm fine, Isak," Tuva insisted. "I will crawl toward the wall and meet you there."

Isak stared at her, and she could see he was struggling to decide what to do. She motioned for him to go ahead, and he started crossing the room toward the seating area.

The ship rocked, the wind howled, and continuous flashes of light burst outside the window. With every list, Tuva feared it might break in two. She finally made it to her destination and curled up against the solid structure. Adam was right behind and crowded next to her, while Isak crawled past her toward the bed.

"What are you doing?" Tuva hollered above the noise.

"I'm grabbing the blankets," Isak yelled. "We're not sure how long this storm will last, and I don't want to have to maneuver around again if I don't have to."

Tuva glanced outside as a flash lit up the sky. It was followed by thunder and another creak of the ship. She flinched, rung her hands, breathed in and out, but felt like she was losing the battle to calm her fears. She continued to watch the raging storm and tried to sway with the motion until Isak's strong arm wrapped around her, holding her firm.

"You, okay?" Isak asked as he stared into her eyes.

"I'm fine," Tuva said. "I'm scared, but I can't do anything about that. I just need to wait it out."

Isak nodded and threw the blankets on the chair next to her.

The three huddled together until Tuva's head bobbed, and she started to drift off to sleep. Her eyes popped open at a loud crash from somewhere and the ship tilted at a dangerous angle. It started to roll onto its side and Tuva tumbled into Adam with Isak knocking into her. Isak's arm snaked around her waist and Adam hugged them both.

"At least we are together if we perish," Adam shouted above the noise.

"I'm so glad you are my wife, Tuva," Isak wailed.

"I care for you so much, Isak," Tuva shrieked. "And, Adam, you have become my brother."

The boat shifted again, and Tuva rammed into her husband, followed by Adam. Adam and Isak tightened their grips, and they all crowded together.

"This is it," Isak hollered. "I love you, brother. I love you both."

Tuva looked into her husband's eyes at his words. She wanted to believe him, but wondered if this was just one of those things people say as they face their last moments before slipping into the ocean. She didn't let her thoughts stay there. She reflected on her parents and sister, and suddenly shouted, "Goodbye," before burying her face into her husband's shoulder.

She allowed herself to be held until the ship listed further, and they tumbled together across the room, slamming into the opposite wall. Isak and Adam instinctively reached for Tuva. She screamed and closed her eyes, and they huddled together, waiting for their end.

Chapter Five

Dear Nora,

Spring has turned into summer here. I know my last letter mostly spoke of our scary passage over, the difficulty in getting settled here, and the harsh winter. I didn't mention much of where we are. New York is such a large city. It is beautiful in some places, but it isn't so pretty where we have been staying. We have been housed together with other families in tiny quarters divided only by paper-thin walls. But the three of us are together, and Isak and Adam were able to drum up enough work to keep us afloat and not use any of the money sent for our travels.

We have secured the train tickets and the rest of the preparations to take us to the Minnesota Territory. We are finally moving on from here. We board the train tomorrow and will take it as far as possible. The rest of the way is on a stagecoach. I am looking forward to being on the last leg of our journey, and, of course, finally getting there. I will write when we are settled.

Give all my love to Mamma and Pappa,

Tuva

Chapter Six

Minnesota Territory 1856

Tuva stared at the passing countryside and struggled to keep her eyes open. They were on the last stretch of their stagecoach ride, and she couldn't wait to finally meet her in-laws. Isak had shared many stories of how his parents had met, fell in love, and created a beautiful life together. He had also explained how their decision to move to America was to give their children a better life. She felt prepared to meet her new family and was excited to see her home after hearing his stories.

The sound of a wagon passing by made Tuva jolt and Isak chuckled. "You should just rest, my love."

"But I don't want to miss anything."

"Adam will wake soon, so perhaps you should rest until he wakes up."

"Maybe I will," Tuva said, letting her eyes close. She leaned against her husband and allowed sleep to take over. Tuva woke suddenly when Adam jolted awake, slamming his knees into her legs.

"Oh. I'm sorry," Adam said.

Isak smacked his brother's leg. "Clumsy oaf."

"Hey, I said I was sorry," Adam said.

"Boys," Tuva said as she put a hand in between the two and laughed. "I'm fine. I need to wake up anyway. We are slowing, which means we are almost there."

Tuva turned her attention back to the window, and her grin widened. The long journey was coming to an end. She was ready for a hot bath and a warm bed in her new home.

The stage slowed to a stop, and she thought her heart would pound out of her chest. They'd arrived in Taylors Falls, but they wouldn't be staying there. They were to procure a wagon and a few horses for the final part of their trip to the Nilsson farm.

Isak asked Tuva if she wanted to stay the night in Taylors Falls and head out in the morning, but she told him no. She could tell Isak and Adam were just as anxious as she to get there.

"Let's get home," she said.

Tuva discovered that Isak's father, Josef, had arranged for a wagon and horses to be held for them, so purchasing them didn't take long. She helped load the wagon, and they were on their way again.

Isak was following a map Josef had sent and the town soon gave way to countryside.

Marveling at the beauty around her, Tuva couldn't figure out what to gaze at next. Isak kept looking around too, but then would focus on the road again.

Adam rode in the back with the trunks and would holler at them when something captured his eye. It became a game for the three of them, which made the time go by quickly.

Isak passed the Center City settlement and eventually turned on a lane. Tuva could see a white farmhouse in the distance. A matching barn was just off to the right, with a large garden in between. The trees and rolling hills of the property were breathtaking.

Tuva noticed a woman walk from the rear of the farmhouse. The woman stopped and held her hand above her eyes as though to get a better look. She let out a shriek and hollered something that was lost in the wind.

Isak had the horses pick up the pace, and the wagon barreled into the farmyard before halting abruptly.

Isak and Adam jumped to the ground and wrapped their arms around the woman who was crying out, "My boys, my boys are finally home."

A lump formed in Tuva's throat, and she instantly missed her own mother. She tried to push away her sadness and focus instead on the joyful reunion of her husband's family.

Tuva started to climb down from her seat, but Isak must have caught sight of her, because his arms engulfed her waist, and he lifted her to the ground. He hugged her and whispered, "We are here."

She beamed at him and followed to meet her mother-in-law.

"Mamma, meet my Tuva. Tuva, this is my mamma, Marriam," Isak said.

"Finally, we get to meet you, my daughter," Marriam said.

"It's such a pleasure," Tuva said, as she held out her hand.

Marriam hugged Tuva, saying, "We hug in this family."

When she pulled away, she turned to her boys, asking them questions about their journey. Tuva looked around the farm and wondered if they would all fit in the small house. It was beautiful, though, and she couldn't wait to go inside.

A slight movement in the fields caught Tuva's attention. "Isak, is that your father and brother?"

She made sure Isak saw where she was pointing, before looking back toward the field. The movement turned into two men running toward them. Tuva grinned at the excitement, but was a little envious at the love and relationship the family obviously had. It was so different from her relationship with her own father, which often tainted the relationship she had with her mother.

She stood back, observing the Nilsson family revel at being together again. Brothers clapped backs, father and sons hugged, and tears flowed freely. Their reunion was the most beautiful thing Tuva had ever seen.

Josef noticed Tuva, and introductions were made all around. More hugs and laughter ensued as Tuva was caught up in the melee.

She started to feel lightheaded, so was thankful when Marriam finally said, "Let's all go inside. What a long journey you have had."

"Come, I will escort you in, Tuva," Isak's youngest brother said. "And you can call me Wally, even though Isak said my name is Walter."

Tuva linked her arm with Wally and beamed up at him. He was quite a bit younger than his oldest brother, but he was the tallest. He was always smiling, with a twinkle of mischief in his eyes, and Tuva loved him instantly.

They walked into the house and as Tuva let her eyes adjust to the room, her earlier concerns of how they would fit rose even higher. The house was clean and tidy, but there were only four chairs at the kitchen table and two rocking chairs by the fire. Off the main room, which consisted of the kitchen and living room area, were two bedrooms. There were stairs leading up to a small loft area, which was open to the great room. A door was nestled in the back of the kitchen. One could see the entire home from the front door.

Tuva complimented the space, but Marriam waved her hand in the air, cutting her off. "We know it's a tight fit, but we won't be living like this for long. We hope to add on to the place eventually or build a second home for you and Isak."

"It's lovely just the same," Tuva said.

"The boys will sleep in the loft. Isak and you will have the room on the left, Tuva," Marriam said, picking up one of the bags and walking in that direction.

Tuva followed and thanked Marriam for getting the room prepared.

"I want you to feel welcome here," Marriam said. "I know what it is like to move to a strange land, and I wanted to make sure this space was pretty for you. If nothing else but to make you feel a little less homesick."

Isak walked into the room with one of the trunks in tow and Tuva followed Marriam back out to the living area.

"Sit," Marriam said, motioning toward one of the rocking chairs. "It's best we stay out of the way while the men bring in the rest of your things. Then you and

I can work on getting supper started. I think it will be an early to bed kind of evening."

Marriam's prediction was correct. It wasn't long after dinner, the whole family turned in for the night. Tuva fell asleep as soon as her head hit the pillow. She wasn't sure what the following day would bring, but she was thankful she was no longer traveling.

Chapter Seven

Tuva woke to her body shaking and she rolled over to see why. She tried to focus on Isak and realized he was calling her name.

"Do you smell that, Tuva?" Isak asked.

"Smoke." Tuva shot up. They threw their covers aside and ran to the bedroom door. When Isak flung open the door, smoke billowed toward them, and flames leapt from the floor and walls in the main room.

"Fire!" Isak shouted.

From above, Adam and Wally cried out, shuffled around, and carefully climbed down from the loft. They had a few items in tow as they ran outside. Isak ran into his parents' bedroom and Tuva went back into their room. She shoved the window open, grabbed as many items as she could, and threw them into the closest travel bag.

Isak ran in behind her. "We have to get out now, Tuva. Quick, climb out the window."

Tuva grabbed the quilt from the bed as she ran past it and climbed out the window. Isak threw the bag, almost hitting Tuva, who had fallen to the ground. Isak grabbed one of the trunks still packed from their journey and hoisted it through the window. It contained a mixture of Tuva and Isak's things, and Tuva was thankful for his quick thinking.

Tuva stood and wrapped the quilt around her body. Isak carried the trunk far enough away to keep it from getting burned and stacked the bag on top. He ran over to her, grabbed her hand, and they charged around to the front of the house.

Isak hurried to help his brothers and father carry buckets to throw water on the house, but they quickly gave up. The fire had grown too big and there was no stopping it. Tuva watched her future burn before her eyes.

The family huddled together, watching the blaze build and consume any remnants of the house. A few items were able to be saved, but not many. Their new home and most of their belongings were gone.

Isak's arm gently draped around Tuva's shoulders, and she leaned against him.

What are we going to do now?

"We will figure this out, I promise," Isak whispered, breaking into her thoughts. She turned to look into his face, and his pained expression broke Tuva's heart.

"Yes," Tuva whispered back, "We will figure this out together."

A month had passed since the fire and Tuva was trying not to give up hope. They had stayed with their neighbors, the Lindstrom's, for a few days, but Josef had insisted it was all the charity the family would take. He and the boys prepared the barn for them to sleep and live while they figured out what was next.

Isak went out every day trying to find work. He discovered a few odd jobs here and there, but nothing lasted for long. Adam and Wally helped their father clean up the charred pile from the fire and Tuva helped Marriam with the cooking, washing, and vegetable garden. It was nearing the end of summer and Tuva became increasingly concerned about how they would survive the winter in a barn.

Tuva gathered her finds from the garden and started to walk toward the barn when Isak's horse pounded down the lane. She looked in his direction and picked up her pace. He was home early, and she feared he would be bringing bad news.

Isak slowed his horse to a stop and jumped to the ground. He was grinning from ear to ear.

"What's going on?" Tuva asked.

"I want to share it with everyone at once if that's okay," Isak said.

"Okay," Tuva said, and helped summon the rest of the family.

When everyone was gathered, Tuva said, "Isak apparently has some news that he wants to share with all of us."

Isak laughed. "Tuva is irritated that I didn't tell her first."

Her cheeks flamed and she gave her husband a pointed look, but smiled when Marriam nodded at her, as though she understood why she would be irritated.

"Well, what is it, boy?" Josef asked. "I have work to get back to."

"Not anymore, Father," Isak said. "That is not if you don't want to."

"I don't understand," Tuva said.

"I have been given some information on where we can start over. It's a place here in Minnesota but along a great lake. One of the men I have been working with gave me this information and he and I looked more into it, and I got us some land. A lot of it. We can start our own copper mine. It's an opportunity for us to start anew and build something special. Something different than what we have done before."

"Have you lost your mind, son?" Marriam said. "I have heard of this great lake. It is cold, and harsh, and the land is difficult."

"Perhaps, but we can start something there. Something that can grow into something bigger," Isak said. He turned to look directly at Tuva. "I just know it."

Tuva studied her husband. "I'm with you, Isak."

Josef left the circle and walked over to the remnants of the home he built. He studied it as he ran his fingers through his graying hair before walking back over to the circle.

"We can sell our little plot here, I suppose, and invest in this new venture."

"You mean that?" Isak asked.

"I do, son."

Marriam cried out, threw her hands in the air, and stomped back to the barn. Tuva followed behind her mother-in-law and let her eyes adjust. She found Marriam leaning against the wall with her face in her hands.

"Marriam, what is it?" Tuva asked.

"This place we are going is not an easy place to live. It is a wilderness and I fear for us. I fear for all of us."

The wind picked up, whistling through the walls. A boom echoed through the room. Tuva jumped, as a shiver ran down her spine, before realizing the barn door had blown shut. She caught a glimpse of her husband through the window. He was huddled with the other men, and she wondered at the decision he had just made for all of them. For the first time in their journey, she could not shake the fear welling up inside her, and she wanted to flee back to Sweden.

Chapter Eight

Dear Nora,

I know I should have written sooner to let you know we made it to the Minnesota Territory, but so much has happened. Mamma was right when she said expect nothing, for it will be an adventure. What an adventure it has been so far. Our new home here is gone, but we have a plan. But that plan means we are moving again. We set out in the morning to start more traveling. Once we are settled, I will write again.

Give Mamma and Pappa all my love,

Tuva

Chapter Nine

The wagon rumbled along the dirt road leading down the side of the mountain and into the small town below. Tuva stared at the blue of the water in the distance before it disappeared behind trees. She turned to look back toward her in-laws and noticed a smile on Marriam's face for the first time in weeks. Tuva knew it was because one could not look at such great beauty and not smile.

She looked forward and helped guide her husband along the bumpy terrain. It wasn't long before they were pulling into the small settlement of Duluth.

"Are you sure this isn't an ocean?" Tuva asked. "It reminds me so much of the water we crossed."

"It isn't, but it's like a small ocean, I have been told. It is a great lake for sure," Isak said as he halted his horses in front of a small building. He hopped off the wagon, said he would be right back, and disappeared into the tiny structure. A few minutes later, he emerged with a smile.

He climbed back on top of the wagon and said, "My friend came through for us. We have a place to stay until we can head up to our land."

Isak pushed the horses on and they rode toward the edge of town before stopping in front of a home smaller than the farmhouse.

Tuva asked, "Are we all staying here?"

"This is just for now, Tuva. You and my parents will stay here while my brothers and I scout our new home."

"You're going to leave me here?"

"I didn't want to concern you with that yet, because I didn't want to scare you," Isak said.

"I'm not scared, Isak. I'm mad," she said. "I'm mad that you don't share with me your plans for our future, and you spring them on me all the time. You don't give me a chance to share my thoughts about anything."

"But I'm your husband. I'm supposed to take care of you," he said with a confused expression.

"A woman doesn't have a thought or an opinion, I suppose," she said, shaking with anger.

"That's not what I meant," Isak said. "But I suppose in some cases a woman's thoughts and opinions should be considered."

Tuva threw her hands in the air and started to climb down from the wagon. Isak told her to wait, and he would help her, but she smacked his hand away and climbed down, muttering, "I'm not a little woman who can't climb off a wagon, Isak. I think it's time you got to know your wife."

Straightening herself out after climbing down, Tuva stomped into the little shack and slammed the door behind her. She couldn't see anything, and she wondered at her surroundings. She probably should have attempted to prove her point a different way. She stumbled around in the dark until she found the shutters to the window and threw them open.

Isak was still sitting on the wagon, staring at the front door with a look of wonderment and confusion. She noticed when he caught sight of her, and his face broke into a wide grin.

He hopped off the wagon and went into the house. "Woman," Isak said. "You amaze me every day."

"Well, you frustrate me most days, Man," Tuva hissed.

Isak laughed out right and wrapped his arms around her.

"I will try and do better about communicating with you," he said, before kissing her soundly.

Tuva thought about rejecting his advances, but she couldn't stay mad at him. She deepened the kiss before pulling away. She swatted him on the rear as she walked past him.

Isak howled louder and went back outside, saying, "I will start unloading."

Tuva got a closer look at their quarters and pushed up her sleeves. They had work to do to make it neat enough for the night. She shook her head and went back outside to help unload the wagons.

The flame burst out from the match as Tuva leaned it toward the paper and twigs to start the fire in the fireplace. The shack had two beds on one side and a small kitchen area on the other. There wasn't a lot of living space and Tuva knew it would be a challenge for all of them to reside together in even tighter conditions than they'd had before.

Once the fire was going, she glanced at her husband. He was hanging string around the beds to create makeshift walls out of blankets. It was the same trick they had used in the barn. Marriam was mixing some oats and water at the counter. Tuva peered out the window at Josef, Wally, and Adam, who were taking care of the horses in the lean-to next to the shack.

Trunks were stacked against the far wall and Tuva wondered if they could be put to better use as chairs until they could make or procure some.

She was about to mention it when Wally walked in, saying, "There is a chill in the breeze from the lake water this evening. I wonder when we could start getting snow up here?"

"I heard it could be any time," Marriam said.

"I don't think quite yet, Mamma," Isak said. "It is only the end of August. I say we have about two months before we could see the first snowfall. At least, that is what my friend Bill told me."

"The same friend Bill that put this copper idea in your head, no doubt," Marriam said, with a tinge of bitterness in her voice.

"Come on, Mamma," Isak said. "You can't be mad at me too."

"Oh, is Tuva mad at you?" Marriam asked.

"I try to be, but it's hard to stay mad at him," Tuva said.

Marriam's countenance softened as she glanced at Tuva. "The love you apparently have for my son is blinding your judgement I fear."

Tuva giggled and went over to hug her mother-in-law.

They leaned against each other until Tuva pulled back, saying, "I will help with dinner."

"Thank you," Marriam said, and continued stirring the oatmeal.

Reaching for the loaf of bread in the food basket, Tuva said, "Wally, why don't you rearrange the trunks. Bring a couple closer to the kitchen area, put them in a circle. We will use those to sit on while we eat. Then put a couple more at the foot of each bed.

This will make it homier, and not like such a warehouse, I think."

"Good idea, Tuva," Isak said.

She winked at her husband and turned to focus on cutting thin slices of bread. This was the last of the bread until they had an oven or found some at the market and wanted to make sure it lasted as long as possible. She cut three slices, cut those in half, and slathered thick jam on each. She divided them on the plates she'd pulled out and rummaged around for bowls.

"I think the bowls are in the trunk at the bottom of the stack, so we will just put the oatmeal on the plate," Marriam said. "I wasn't thinking clearly when I packed."

"That's okay. Plates will work fine."

The oatmeal was just finishing when Josef walked in with Adam.

"I think everything is secure enough for the night," Josef said. "In the morning, we will go and sell the one wagon and team of horses. We won't need two up here."

Tuva's heart sank at the realization there was no turning back. As Adam started to close the door, she caught sight of the pink reflecting on the water from the setting sun. She walked over to keep Adam from closing the door behind him. She pushed it open further and said, “Look at that.”

The family gathered around Tuva, and she said, “Maybe this isn’t such a bad place after all.”

Marriam snorted. “Beauty can be deceiving.”

“Maybe,” Tuva said, “but I could stare at that beauty for hours.”

Isak held her hand and said, “I hope that never changes.”

Tuva turned to her husband. “And I hope this was a good decision.”

He looked down at her. “I will just make sure it is.”

Chapter Ten

Tuva watched her husband sail away with his brothers and an ache grew in the pit of her stomach. They had only been in Duluth a few days when Isak finalized the arrangements with his friend Bill's help. They purchased a boat to take him and his brothers up to their new land. She was told it would take most of the day for them to get there. But Tuva wouldn't know for at least a month if they arrived safely.

Marriam hugged Tuva to her. "It will be okay, my dear. They will watch out for one another."

Taking a deep breath, Tuva said, "I know, but since the day I said 'I do' to Isak, my life has been ever changing. First it was coming to America, then it was living on the farm, then the house burned, and now I'm in the middle of a northern wilderness and my husband has left me alone."

"But you are not alone. You have me and Josef," Marriam said, "and the next month will go by so fast. I promise."

"I hope so."

"I learned long ago not to expect things and go with the flow in this family," Marriam said.

"Hmm, that is the same philosophy my mother had."

"Wise woman," Marriam said, nudging Tuva gently. "Let's go walk a bit and see if there are any other women in this place."

"You won't find many women about," Josef said. "There are a few, but not a lot. And the ones that are here live in the nicer houses."

"So, they probably won't talk to us poor folk then," Tuva said, sticking her nose in the air.

Marriam giggled. "That's the spirit. Let's at least walk to the market and buy a few items for dinner."

"Sounds good to me," Tuva said.

"I will meet you ladies at home," Josef said, and went off in the direction of their shack.

Tuva and Marriam walked along the dusty roads trying to become more familiar with the small town. The sky was bright blue, the warmth of the sun was glorious on Tuva's face, and she wondered if they should be at home doing the wash instead of strolling along.

"The chores will wait," Marriam said, breaking into Tuva's thoughts.

"How did you know what I was thinking?"

"You are easy to read. Everything you are thinking seems to be written all over your face."

"I guess I'm an open book."

"That's not a bad thing. It just means you're honest."

"I suppose," Tuva said and turned the corner. Her steps faltered when the group walking toward them came into full view. But she refused to play into the stories people often shared. She had always believed one must not judge unless they know firsthand who someone was.

"Should we cross the street?" Marriam asked.

Tuva turned toward her mother-in-law knowing there was surprise written on her face and said, "Why on earth would we do that? Don't be silly. They are just people."

"A native people."

"We shouldn't be so judgmental. Fearing the unknown shouldn't play into our judgements of others. Just the same as other people's fears shouldn't," Tuva said gently and turned back toward the others walking toward them. She tried not to openly stare but couldn't keep from studying them.

The two women wore long tan dresses with beads and other ornaments adorning the sleeves and chest of the gowns. The men wore pants and shirts of the same material, and they all wore the softest looking shoes. The differences in their outfits were beautiful, and Tuva wondered how they created their clothing.

They each carried baskets of goods, and Tuva wondered if they were selling or trading their items.

As they walked past, Tuva smiled, but no one would look her in the eye, save one woman who grinned back. A connection floated between them, and she wondered if the other woman felt the same thing. She hoped she would get the chance to see her again.

Marriam linked arms with her and whispered, "You are right, Tuva, one must not judge."

With a lightness in her step, Tuva walked on to the market with Marriam, hoping the rest of the day would be just as lovely.

Chapter Eleven

The sun began to fall behind the trees and Tuva realized her mistake in taking such a long walk. She had gone farther this time, enjoying the nature and beauty of her surroundings. It had been a week since Isak had left, and she had taken to walking every day to help pass the time. It had also become a way to get to know the people and the area a little better.

She hadn't seen the Ojibwe from before but looked for them often. She really wanted to meet and get to know them. Tuva was thinking of them as she quickened her pace. She walked through the brush along the path she had taken and almost stumbled. She burst out of the trees and her heart calmed a little at the lights of the small town below her. She was almost back.

Tuva rounded a corner in the path and crashed into a man. She fell back, landed on her bottom, and let out a yelp. The man leaned down to help her up and she caught the alcohol on his breath. She allowed the man to help her up, quickly thanked him, apologized for colliding with him, and kept walking along the path.

"Now wait just a minute there, pretty lady," the man said. "Where ya going in such a hurry?"

"I must be getting back to help my family with dinner," she hollered over her shoulder. "Thanks again, and again, my apologies."

The man ran after Tuva and grabbed her arm, yanking her around to face him. "I said wait a minute."

Tuva's stomach lurched as a shudder snaked up her spine.

Warning bells grew louder in her head. "Mister, I must ask that you let me be. My family will come looking for me, any moment if I don't return home soon."

"That just gives me time to get to know you better."

"No, it really doesn't. Now please, let me go."

"Nah, I don't think I will," the man said as he pulled Tuva into a rough and sloppy kiss.

She kicked at the man and squirmed, trying to get out of his grasp, but only managed to move her mouth away from his.

"Leave me be. My husband will be here any second," Tuva lied.

The man tried to kiss her again, and Tuva bit him hard. He let her go for only a second, but it was long enough for her to escape, and she bolted. She quickened her pace, but could hear the man's footsteps thundering behind her. She realized he was slower than she, and thought she could get away, but stumbled on a rock, falling hard to the ground.

Tuva tried to hop back up, but her fall gave the man the chance to catch up, and he dove on top of her. She struggled to get away, but he smacked her in the face a couple of times. Her head spun, her ears rang, and she went limp. The man clawed at the front of her dress, ripping it in several places. He started to pull up her dress, ripping it as it slid higher up her body. This seemed to revive her enough to scream.

The man snickered. "Not a soul gonna hear ya scream, lady."

Tuva's resolve to get away returned, and she hit and kicked with all the strength she had left. With every blow against him, he was able to block the next and smack her just as hard. She was losing the battle.

Her stomach roiled and bile burned in the back of Tuva's throat as the realization of what was about to happen settled in. She tried to reposition her legs, but he forced them apart with his thighs. He fumbled with the front of his pants, and she tried once more to scream. But he cut her off with his fist.

While the man continued his attack on her body, she struggled to digest what was happening. Tuva detached as though she were floating above them and could only watch in horror.

There was a rustle in the trees, and two figures appeared, knocking the man off Tuva. She rolled away, jumped, and started to run, but tripped again. Tuva stumbled and froze. She realized she was surrounded by the same Ojibwe she had met on the road the week prior.

She looked back just in time to see her attacker being bound and pushed to a sitting position. The woman Tuva thought she had connected with walked into the light of the setting sun and asked, "You okay?"

Tuva burst into tears and sank to the ground.

The woman reached over and patted Tuva on the shoulder. "You are okay now. We protect you."

"Thank you so much," Tuva said. "I don't know what would have happened if you hadn't arrived."

"I do and I'm glad we are here," the woman said, and helped Tuva to her feet.

Tuva thanked the woman again. "My name is Tuva."

"Minwaadizi."

"What a beautiful name," Tuva said.

The woman said something in her dialect to one of the men standing over her attacker, and he responded in the same language.

"What are you saying?" Tuva asked.

"We will take the man and you to a friend. The friend will take care of the man. Then he will take you to your home."

Tuva nodded and allowed the woman to help her walk. She stumbled occasionally as they walked along the path into town. Minwaadizi helped steady her when needed and made sure she was okay to continue.

When they arrived at the friend's house, he came out, and the men huddled together. Tuva could hear them talking between glances her way. When the attack was mentioned, the friend held up his hand and called for another man to come out of the house, who took her attacker into a barn, while the friend walked toward her.

He paused, studying her closely, before wrapping a coat around her shoulders. "What's your name, miss?"

"My name is Tuva Nilsson. That man attacked me."

"Yes, that is what Makwa said," the man paused. "I'm Bill. A friend of your husband's."

Nervous laughter bubbled inside Tuva.

She knew she sounded hysterical, saying, "Of course you are. I don't know if I should hug you or hit you, Bill. You put ideas in my husband's head and now I'm alone here in this wilderness getting attacked."

"I'm sorry, Mrs. Nilsson," he said. "Truly I am."

Tuva waved her hand. "I don't care about that right now. I just want to get back to my little home and clean up. I'm sure I look a mess."

"Of course." Bill turned to Makwa and said, "She appears to be in some shock. I will see her home. You head out now. And we will take care of the trash later."

Makwa nodded, said something Tuva couldn't understand, and turned to leave.

"Wait," Tuva said. "Please, I just want to thank you again. Minwaadizi, thank you."

Minwaadizi smiled and nodded, a sadness in her eyes, and whispered, "Goodbye."

Tuva watched them go while Bill grabbed a lantern. The sun was well below the trees now and a faint hue of pink glistened in the distance, but it wasn't enough light to guide the way. Tuva let Bill escort her home and neither of them spoke until they arrived.

"Thank you for your assistance," Tuva said, as the front door flung open.

"Tuva, there you are," Josef said. "We were getting worried."

Marriam appeared behind her husband and asked, "Are you okay, dear?"

"I'm a little banged up, but I'm okay now," Tuva said, standing in the shadows. "Just tired and could really use a bath."

"She was attacked by a local troublemaker who we will finally be able to ship out of here," Bill said.

"Attacked," Marriam shrieked, and pulled Tuva into the house. "Let me get a better look at you."

Tuva tried to relax under the scrutiny and wondered what she must look like as a look of horror crossed Marriam's face.

"Gracious, child. What happened? Who did this? Do you even want to talk about it right now?" Marriam asked.

"I walked a little too far and was attacked by a man," Tuva said. "I was saved by the people we saw the other day and they took me to Bill's house."

"Who is Bill?" Josef asked.

"I'm Bill," Bill said, raising his hand in the air with a small wave.

"He is the same Bill who is Isak's friend," Tuva said.

"Can I see this man who attacked our daughter?" Josef asked.

"No, please," Tuva said. "I just want to get cleaned up and rest. I just want this all to just go away."

Marriam studied Tuva before she leaned in, whispering, "Did he try to do something to you, Tuva?"

Tuva stared at her mother-in-law, trying to figure out what to say when Bill spoke up. "I think I'll be heading out now. I'll come by later tomorrow to make sure you're all okay if that works for you."

"That's just fine. Thank you," Josef said.

Once the door closed behind Bill, Tuva walked over to her bed to lie down. Marriam must have followed, because her hand rested on Tuva's shoulder. Tuva flinched and Marriam let go.

"Tuva, I'm worried for you. Are you okay?"

"I think I'm a little in shock or something. I just want to clean up and rest," Tuva said.

"Of course, dear. Josef, prepare a hot bath, then go down to the pub for a couple of hours," Marriam directed.

Josef obeyed his wife, and pulled the tub out from the corner, then started heating water on the stove. He made several trips to fill the tub fuller than he usually did.

When he was done, Josef said, "I think it's ready. I left a kettle of water to keep warm on the stove, if you need more hot water."

"Thank you, dear," Marriam said.

Josef nodded once, looked over at Tuva and started to say something, but must have thought better of it, because he put on his hat and left. Tuva rose to a sitting position after the front door closed, and she asked Marriam to lock it for her.

Marriam nodded and went to secure the door while Tuva started to undress. As she pulled the fragments of her garment off her shoulder, she winced and glanced at it. It was turning a purple hue and she realized she might have more bruises on her body than she thought, so took her time taking the rest of her clothes off.

Once in the water, Tuva curled up and closed her eyes, allowing the warmth of the water to envelop her.

"Do you want to talk about it?" Marriam asked.

Tuva sat quietly. She was trying to figure out what to say or whether she even wanted to say anything. She let out a sigh and said, "I was walking and ran into a man. He tried to force himself on me. I tried to fight him off. I was losing until the people came, and they saved me."

"The Ojibwe?" Marriam asked. "Did he, well you know, um did he ..." Marriam trailed off.

"He wasn't able to complete what he was trying to do."

Sighing in relief, Marriam whispered, "How horrible, my daughter. I'm so sorry this happened to you."

Marriam sat down on the nearest trunk and stared toward the kitchen. Tuva closed her eyes, thankful the conversation seemed to be over, and sank further into the water, hoping it would get rid of the filth covering her body.

The shadows in the small home changed, signaling the sun was completely gone now, giving way to the darkness of the night. Tuva adjusted herself in the bath and started to clean her body. She winced while cleaning her face, so she skimmed her fingers gently over the area to assess the damage. Her eyes were swollen, and the cuts on her lips stung as she passed over them.

Tears welled up in the corners of Tuva's eyes when Marriam asked, "May I help you with washing your hair?"

"Yes, I would like that," Tuva whispered, trying to maintain her composure at the gentleness and care she was receiving after such a traumatic experience.

Tuva leaned forward, closing her eyes at the cool touch of her mother-in-law's fingers. Marriam poured warm water over her hair and massaged soap onto her scalp. Stiffness eased slightly from Tuva's shoulders.

Marriam cleared her throat. "I was attacked once. Josef knows about this. But my boys don't know about it. He was successful, but thankfully no baby came of it. Josef and I had only been married a couple of months when it happened. Shortly after that, we moved from the city to our little home in the country, and that was when I started to feel safe again."

Tuva listened intently. She could feel the pain and heartache her mother-in-law spoke of.

"I'm so sorry," Tuva whispered.

"And I'm sorry for you, Tuva," Marriam said. "To be attacked in this way ... it takes something from you."

Tuva wondered at Marriam's words and worried that she would never feel safe or normal again, but she mostly felt numb and ached for that to ease.

"It is a dark thing to happen to someone," Marriam said.

"Is it okay if we do not speak on this again? Or at least until I'm ready?" Tuva asked. "I don't want Isak to know. He is so intent on protecting me that I worry about him ... if he was to find out I was attacked."

Marriam patted Tuva's head. "Of course, we will keep our secrets close, and I will tell Josef to not say anything either."

Marriam finished washing Tuva's hair and helped her out of the bath. Tuva tried to ignore the looks of horror and pain from Marriam as she handed Tuva a towel before turning away. Tuva surveyed the bruises all over her body and shuddered.

Once she dried off and dressed, Marriam offered to brush her hair, and Tuva nodded her agreement. They didn't speak the rest of the evening, and when Tuva went to bed, she forced all thoughts of her attack out of her mind. Instead, while she drifted off to sleep, she focused on the gentleness and care she'd received from her in-laws.

The night would not be a blissful one, though. She tossed and turned and dreamed of men's hands clawing at her body.

Chapter Twelve

Tuva jumped at the knock on the front door. She turned and froze while the wash rag dripped suds and dish water on the floor. She wasn't sure if she should flee or hide.

"Are you okay?" Marriam asked.

Tuva shook her head but said, "Yes, that just startled me."

"It's understandable that your nerves would be on edge still," Marriam said, as she crossed to answer the door.

When Marriam flung the door open, Bill stood with his fist raised like he was about to knock again. Tuva's spirits lifted at the sight of him, and she dropped the dishrag into the basin of water and quickly dried her hands. Bill had come every day since her attack, and she had begun to look forward to his visits.

Marriam frowned and looked over at Tuva. "Bill's here. Again."

Tuva could tell her mother-in-law was uncomfortable with how often Bill had been by to check on her, but she didn't care. She was thankful for the distraction, and for someone else to talk to.

Bill crossed to sit at the kitchen table, and Tuva sat across from him. She knew if she was any closer, it would be considered improper. She wondered if his constant visits were unconventional, but she always pushed that thought out of her head since she was still wounded, and trying to recover from her attack. He treated her like she wasn't fragile. He treated her like she was normal, and she knew she couldn't heal without that.

"What news do you have for me today?" she asked.

Bill rung his hands, looked past her, then down at his feet.

"You are making me nervous, Bill," Tuva said. "Is it Isak?"

"Oh gosh, no. It isn't Isak," he said. "I just wasn't sure if I should share the news, is all."

"The news about what?" Marriam asked, sitting next to Tuva.

"I thought maybe you should know. The man that attacked you. Well, he escaped last night," Bill said.

Tuva felt vomit lurch up, and her heart pounded so hard she thought it would beat its way out of her chest. "No, that can't be."

"Yes, I'm afraid so," he said.

"What are you doing about it?" Marriam asked, placing her hand on Tuva's shoulder.

"Nothing I can do. It's up to the authorities. I know they are investigating as to where he would have gone. And they have searched for him, but haven't found him or any clues yet."

Tuva shoved away from the table and walked over to the window to stare out at the blue of the water. The view always helped calm her heart and mind, and she needed that peace now more than ever.

"Do they think he is hiding somewhere around here?" Marriam asked.

"No, and maybe that will help put your mind at ease," Bill said. "They think he left town. Just not sure if he went south back toward Minneapolis or further north."

Tuva turned and looked over at Bill. "You're confident he is gone?"

Bill stood and crossed to Tuva. He placed a hand on her shoulder and examined her eyes so long it almost made Tuva uncomfortable.

Marriam cleared her throat.

Bill said, "I swear to you that I believe he is gone."

Tuva turned back toward the view, biting her lip, and nodded her head. *That will have to do. He can't hurt you now, Tuva,* she tried to reassure herself.

"You staying for lunch today, Bill?" Marriam asked, changing the subject.

"I can't today," he said. "But I will be back to check on things another day."

Marriam thanked him for coming and Tuva knew her mother-in-law was relieved he was leaving. Tuva called a farewell, but couldn't turn away from the water until the door shut, signaling he was gone.

"I know you don't like that he visits so much," Tuva said.

"I think it isn't proper for a single man to be visiting a married woman is all," Marriam said. "But I allow it due to the circumstances."

"I wish we would have been able to get to know more people," Tuva said. "With the attack, I have had a hard time venturing out again."

"That is understandable," Marriam said. "Which is why I allow his visits. I just caution you."

"I know," Tuva said, and looked back out the window. "I miss Isak so much."

"We all do, my dear," Marriam said. She walked over and gently put her arm around Tuva. "You have been through so much in such a short amount of time. Perhaps maybe you should write your sister. Let her know she can finally write you here."

Tuva brightened. "That is a great idea. I will do that later this evening."

Marriam turned back to her chores while Tuva stared out at the lake, pushing the conversation of her attacker escaping out of her mind. She wrestled with her thoughts until she was calm again and knew she could carry on.

Chapter Thirteen

Dear Nora,

I'm sorry I haven't written sooner. So much has happened. We are settled in the new town of Duluth on this great lake. It reminds me so much of the ocean. The blue of it changes with each passing moment of the day, and I could stare at it forever. Isak is getting our home ready for us at our new homestead, where they will be mining copper. I haven't seen or heard from him since he left, and I miss him so. My feelings for him have continued to grow with each passing day. I hope he feels the same about me.

About a month ago, I was attacked by a terrible man. Isak doesn't know, and I don't want him to. I was saved by some new friends. They are from the Ojibwe tribe. They are the most wonderful of people. I also met Isak's friend, Bill. He visits us often while Isak is gone.

I miss you, dear sister. It gets quite lonely here sometimes.

Don't tell Mamma or Pappa about my attack.

You can write to me here.

Tuva

Chapter Fourteen

Tuva carried the bucket of water from the lake up toward her small home when she caught sight of Bill walking toward the little shack. He looked nervous and distracted and didn't seem to notice when Tuva waved in his direction. He knocked at the door, but with no answer, he spun around and started to walk back the way he had come until he spotted Tuva.

"Bill, you look a bit flustered. Are you okay?" Tuva asked.

"Yes, and, no," he said.

"Are you going to explain to me what this is about?" Tuva asked. "Is it Isak? My attacker?"

"No, neither of those. It's just the owners of your shack are coming back, and they want to move in next week."

Tuva stopped and placed the bucket at her feet. "I'm confused. I thought Isak bought this place."

"He paid for four months' rent," Bill said. "The owners had said they were not planning to return until next spring, so I thought it would be okay, but they decided to return before the winter hit."

"Marriam and Josef ran to the market but will be back shortly. Why don't you come in as they will be returning soon, and you can help us figure out what to do next," Tuva offered.

"I do have a couple of ideas, just not great ones," he said.

"Well, since we will be homeless next week, any idea is better than no idea," Tuva said, picking up the bucket and carrying it to the front door.

Bill ran to grab the bucket from her. His hand brushed hers, jostling the bucket, and water splashed out.

"You got it?" Tuva asked.

Looking surprised, Bill nodded and walked into the house ahead of Tuva.

I caution you, flitted through Tuva's head, but she pushed aside those thoughts and kept them at bay. She was, after all, a married woman, and Bill was her husband's friend. She knew she didn't have those types of feelings for Bill, but for the first time started to worry about the situation.

Tuva turned toward boots crunching on gravel to find Marriam and Josef walking toward her. Their arms were laden with goods from the market. Relief flooded through her. She was thankful they had arrived before being in the little home by herself with another man who was not her husband. She trusted

Bill, but she had trouble being around any man alone since her attack.

"Bill is here," Tuva said, grabbing a few items out of Marriam's arms. "He says we have to move."

"What is this?" Josef asked.

"You better come in, and he will explain it to you," Tuva said, following her in-laws into the house.

Bill explained the circumstances to the Nilssons and then offered two prospects. One option was residing with him, since he had extra space. The other was staying in an even smaller shack on the other side of town, closer to the woods than the lake.

"I could stay in the barn if that would make you feel more comfortable," Bill said.

Tuva couldn't stomach the thought of living so close to the woods where she was attacked, but after Bill's reaction to brushing his hand against hers, she was worried about his other suggestion as well. She looked over at her in-laws to see their reactions and caught Marriam studying her. Josef pushed his chair away from the table and started to pace back and forth across the small space.

"What do you think, Marriam?" Tuva asked.

"I know being close to those woods would be difficult for Tuva, but the alternative ..."

Tuva knew Marriam was concerned about Bill being near Tuva all the time. Before today, Tuva wouldn't have thought anything of it. But now she wasn't sure it would be such a good idea either.

"Josef, what are your thoughts?" Tuva asked.

"I don't like living off of charity, but I don't want you to be uncomfortable, Tuva."

"You will be getting some of your rent money back, so I could just transfer part of it to me, if that would make you feel better," Bill said.

Tuva avoided looking in Bill's direction and instead studied Marriam and Josef. She couldn't be the one to make this decision, but she was terrified of either outcome.

Marriam stood slowly and walked over to look out the window. The room grew quiet. Josef stopped pacing and watched his wife. Tuva was sure everyone could hear the banging of her heart while she waited for a decision to be made.

Looking over her shoulder at Tuva, Marriam said, "I think we don't have a choice right now. We will rent from Bill, but only if he stays in the barn."

Bill grinned. "I'm so glad we could come up with a solution, and of course I will make space for me in my barn. Oh, and Tuva, you will have a lovely view of your water."

Tuva glanced over at Bill. Her cheeks grew warm at how intimately Bill spoke to her about her love of the lake. She looked back toward Marriam, and they exchanged a look while *I caution you* danced through Tuva's head.

Chapter Fifteen

Tuva watched Marriam study her out of the corner of her eye as she finished the last of the dinner preparations. It was Bill's birthday, and although things had been awkward since moving into his home, she didn't want to appear ungrateful by ignoring his birthday, so had offered to make a special dinner for him.

Marriam helped some, but had cut her hand while slicing vegetables earlier, so couldn't do as much. Josef and Bill were out in the barn doing the last of the evening chores. So, it was all up to Tuva to pull the meal together.

"He is growing very fond of you, Tuva," Marriam said.

Tuva's shoulders slumped as she finished setting the table. "If it makes you feel better, I have grown concerned at his feelings for me too."

"It does at that," Marriam said. "But the heart sometimes cannot stop what grows there."

"I don't care for him, Marriam," Tuva said. "I hope you know that. I hope you believe that."

"I mostly do," Marriam said. "Sometimes, though, like today, offering to make him a special dinner. That could confuse him about your feelings. It confuses me sometimes, but then I don't see you look at him the way you looked at my Isak, and I feel better about it."

"I don't know what to do about it," Tuva said. "He hasn't said anything to me. Or made any advances. Everything we are discussing right now is from what we think is happening without any evidence, really."

"No evidence, you say. I disagree."

"What evidence do you have?" Tuva asked.

"He watches you. He looks at you with longing but then tries to hide it when you look his way."

"That isn't my fault."

"You are correct. It isn't your fault, unless you're encouraging it, or not stopping it," Marriam said.

"This is the first I'm hearing of how he looks at me."

"Well, just be careful."

"I'm," Tuva said. "I'm trying to be."

Footsteps clomping on the front porch alerted Tuva, and she changed the subject to the weather growing colder as Josef and Bill walked in.

"Smells delicious," Josef said.

"Thank you, Josef," Tuva said. "This was one of my pappa's favorite dishes."

"Then I'm sure it will be good," Bill said, while he washed the grime of the chores off his hands.

Josef followed Bill's example, and they all sat around the table, with Bill sitting across from Tuva.

She could tell he was trying not to gape at her, and she glanced over at Marriam, who gave her a pointed look. Tuva shrugged and offered to pass the food around.

The conversation stayed light while they ate, with discussions around the market being busy and the coolness in the air. Josef told a story about a dog and a little boy, which made Tuva and the rest of the table laugh. When everyone was finished eating, she announced she had made a small dessert and pulled it out of its hiding place.

Marriam glanced in Bill's direction, and Tuva wondered what she saw there, because alarm flitted across her face before she looked over at Tuva. Tuva looked at Bill, but he was wiping his mouth with a napkin and looking down at his plate.

She looked back over at Marriam, who shook her head and mouthed, "Caution."

I shouldn't have made the dessert. Too late now.

Tuva cut the cake and dished it out to everyone before saying she was too full, and would start the dinner clean up. She cleared away most of the dishes and was thankful when Josef seemed to occupy Bill's attention by asking questions about tomorrow's chores. Marriam chimed in here and there, but Tuva paid little attention to what they were saying before she snuck out the back door off the kitchen, to catch a glimpse of the setting sun.

What am I to do? Oh, Isak, when will you be back to take us home?

Tuva turned toward footsteps behind her. She was worried it might be Bill, but relief flooded through her body as Marriam approached.

"It's not your fault," Marriam said.

"I know. I just wish Isak was here."

"Me too, my dear. Me too."

"Marriam, can you help me?" Josef hollered from the house.

"Be right there," Marriam said, rolling her eyes. She reached out and cupped her hand under Tuva's chin. "I'm so glad my Isak married you."

Tears sprang into Tuva's eyes while she watched her mother-in-law disappear into the house. She wrapped her arms around herself, and hugged tight, before turning to watch the fading orange on the water. A shiver coursed through her, signaling it was time to go in, and she went back to cleaning the kitchen.

By the time all the dishes were done, and everything was put away, Bill had gone back to the barn. Marriam and Josef sat by the small fire now burning in the fireplace. They were discussing memories of their boys, and Tuva giggled at the antics described in their stories. Their conversation turned to when they first met, and Tuva didn't want to interrupt the beautiful moment her in-laws were sharing, so she grabbed her shawl and snuck out the kitchen door to look at the stars.

The twinkling from the night sky reflected on the lake, and Tuva wondered if Isak was staring at the same thing, thinking of her. She wiped at the moisture on her cheek and pulled her shawl closer to ward off the chill in the night air.

"Are you cold?" Bill asked from behind, and she spun around, startled at his presence. "Sorry, I didn't mean to scare you."

She waved her hand in the air. "No, it's fine. I was just deep in thought, thinking of Isak."

Bill stepped closer, and Tuva noticed he was frowning when he asked, "Do you think of him often?"

"I think about him every day," she said.

"I see."

"What do you see?" Tuva asked, not really wanting to know the answer, but wanting to get this conversation over with.

"Do you love him then?" he asked.

"He is my husband."

"Yes, but do you love him?"

Tuva hesitated, wondering how she should respond. She was devoted to Isak and cared for him on their wedding day, but the word love had never crossed their lips, outside the one time on the ship over when they thought they were going to die. But her feelings for her husband grew more every day, even with his absence.

"You hesitate, so that gives me hope," Bill said, breaking into her thoughts.

"Bill, you must understand that there could never be anything between us."

He took another step closer, bringing him inches from her face.

Tuva's heart began to race, not from wanting the man standing before her, but from not knowing what he was going to do next. Just as she started to take a step back, Bill snaked his arms around her and kissed her passionately. Tuva turned her head away and pushed hard against his chest with both her hands. This knocked them both off balance, and they stumbled away from one another.

"Bill, please," Tuva managed to get out before rushing past him.

Bill grabbed Tuva's arm before she reached the back door. "Please don't go in yet. Allow me the chance to apologize."

Tuva paused but didn't turn around.

"I know I'm a fool to think there could ever be anything between us," Bill began. "I'm sorry I kissed you.

I shouldn't have done that. I will keep my distance for a while so as not to make you feel uncomfortable, but know that I will always be here for you if you ever need anything. As a friend."

"Thank you, Bill. And I'm sorry if I ever did anything to make you think you could kiss me."

"You did nothing. It was all me."

"Well, goodnight then."

"Goodnight," Bill said, and Tuva went into the house.

As she took her shawl off and hung it on its hook, Marriam said, "So, it has been done, then."

"Yes, it has. He knows I don't care for him in that way."

"I noticed you couldn't say you love Isak."

Tuva reflected on how to answer before explaining, "I guess I'm afraid to answer that question for fear he doesn't feel the same about me."

"Of course, he loves you," Marriam said. "He wouldn't have married you if he didn't."

"Maybe, but he has never told me," Tuva said.

"Then he is a fool," Marriam said, and hugged Tuva.

"Thank you for being so understanding about all this," Tuva said. "I don't know what to say to Isak about it, though."

"We will just keep our secrets close," Marriam said.

Tuva melted into her mother-in-law's embrace.

"Come, let's go to bed," Marriam said.

"That sounds wonderful," Tuva said. "I'm exhausted."

Chapter Sixteen

Small white flakes fell from the sky and landed in Tuva's outstretched hand. She watched them melt before brushing her hands together and looking out across the water. She stood on the pebbled beach, wishing she would see a boat bringing her husband back to her. But there were only tiny waves, and the sun glistening through the snowfall.

It had been three months since Isak left, and it was long past the time for him to return to collect her. With each passing day, she became more worried something had happened to him, and she would never see him again.

Tuva caught movement out of the corner of her eye and turned to see what it was, and her face broke into a grin.

"Minwaadizi, hello," Tuva said, as she turned toward her friend. She had seen the Ojibwa woman many times at the market in the last couple of months, and her respect and admiration for her new friend grew with each passing conversation.

"Hello, Tuva," Minwaadizi said. "Watching for your Isak?"

"Yes, I watch for him every day."

“I find watching never makes my Makwa appear.”

“I suppose you’re right.”

“He will return,” Minwaadizi said. “I feel this in my heart.”

“I feel it too. But sometimes I worry about him,” Tuva said.

“Worry will not change the outcome,” Minwaadizi said.

“Again, you are so right,” Tuva said. Changing the subject, she asked, “What brings you down by the lake today? I usually see you at the market at this time.”

“I came to say goodbye to my friend.”

“Goodbye?” Tuva asked. “Where are you going?”

“It is time for us to move on from this place, for the winter at least,” Minwaadizi said.

“So, I may never see you again?”

“This is possible. But I take you with me in my heart. You are a good friend.”

“And you are a good friend to me and will always be in my heart, too.” Tuva paused and tried not to let Minwaadizi read her expression when she asked, “May I give you a hug goodbye?”

“Yes,” Minwaadizi said, and they embraced.

As they pulled apart, Tuva thought she caught a glimpse of the same sentiments in her friend’s eyes, before Minwaadizi waved and walked away. As she watched her friend disappear into the trees, a twinge of pain fractured in her chest, and she wasn't sure how much more heartache she could bear.

Tuva faced the water. The words, "Oh Isak," whispered across the waves before she too walked from the beach back toward home.

As she neared the house, Marriam came out and said, "I was beginning to worry. You were gone longer than normal."

"I was saying goodbye to Minwaadizi," Tuva said. "They are leaving, and I will probably never see her again."

"Oh, Tuva, I know how much you have grown fond of one another," Marriam said. "Come inside and let me get you some coffee while you warm by the fire."

"That would be lovely."

Marriam bustled around the kitchen preparing the hot beverage while Tuva warmed her hands by the crackling flames. Tuva tried to keep her thoughts from wandering, so as not to worry about Isak again. Marriam brought steaming mugs for both and sat opposite her.

They sipped in silence until Marriam clumsily placed her cup on the table next to her, saying, "Goodness, where is my mind? I almost forgot."

Pulling a small envelope from her apron pocket, Marriam said, "This came for you today. I believe it might be from Nora."

Tuva placed her coffee next to her and gingerly held the letter so she could read the front of it. "Oh," Tuva said as she hugged the envelope to her chest.

Marriam gathered her mug and stood. "I will leave you to it."

"Thank you." Tuva watched her mother-in-law walk away. Once Marriam was out of sight, she tore into the envelope and pulled out the letter.

Dear Tuva,

Your letters have been so irregular, but I cling to each one as a reminder that you are still alive and, despite the trials and adventures, are doing well. Your northern wilderness and great lake sound wonderful, and I worry about you being alone without your Isak. But I find comfort in your in-laws being there to help you.

Mamma has been ill, but I believe she is finally on the mend. And Pappa, well, you know how he is. He never changes. Just when I think I might find favor with him, he brushes me aside. But enough about them. I met a boy. He is so handsome, and he has so many dreams. I think he might want to marry me some day. Mamma says I'm too young. But Pappa says, one less mouth to feed, so we will see what happens. I'm sorry of your attack. I did not tell our parents.

I miss you desperately, sister.

All my love,

Nora

Tuva read the letter a few more times before staring into the fire. She let her mind wander to her childhood home. She had been gone for over a year, yet it seemed like a lifetime since she had been there. She let her tears fall unchecked as she thought about her sister and missing the wedding she was sure would be happening soon.

A flash of a memory came to mind, and she ran across the room, pushed aside her makeshift blanket wall, and flung open her trunk. She dug around until her hand brushed against wood. Smiling, she gently pulled the picture out from under a blanket. She was thankful it had been in the trunk that was saved from the fire.

Tuva stared at her family until Marriam walked over to stand next to her.

"I'm okay," Tuva said. "Just missing them. But I'm okay."

Marriam mumbled something about dinner but to come whenever she was ready, and Tuva listened to her footsteps fade away. Tuva sat on her bed and held the picture to her chest, thinking of her childhood and the antics her and Nora always got in trouble for.

She wasn't sure how long she sat there, but Josef and Bill coming in for dinner indicated it had been too long. She decided she couldn't mope forever, so wrapped the frame back up and placed it in the trunk. Tuva patted the trunk, then straightened her shoulders and went to eat. It was a quiet supper, and she didn't say much as she concentrated on her plate of food.

At one point, Josef asked if Tuva was okay. She was thankful that Marriam responded for her, explaining it had been a long day for Tuva and she was just tired.

Josef glanced from his wife to Tuva, shrugged his shoulders, and went back to eating his dinner. Tuva tried to ignore the look of concern Bill had every time he looked her way, and was thankful when everyone finished eating. She didn't like the attention, especially with the way things had gone with Bill and her missing Isak.

Once the dishes were cleared, Bill retired to the barn for the night, and Josef went to sit in his rocking chair. Tuva tried to help with the rest of the cleanup, but Marriam wouldn't have it. She told Tuva to go sit by the fire and rest. Thankful for a break, Tuva gathered a pen and paper with every intention of writing her sister, but found herself getting lost in the warmth of the flames.

Marriam finished cleaning the kitchen and made her way to the fireplace, where Josef stood to give her his seat. As Marriam settled, several footsteps rustled on the front porch, followed by a bang on the door. Tuva flinched and wondered at who could be there so late in the evening. Her first thought was of the attacker coming back, but then realized if it was him, he wouldn't knock.

Josef opened the door slowly, before flinging it open. "Saints be praised."

Tuva and Marriam moved toward the door, as three men with beards rushed into the room. Tuva locked eyes with one of the men. "Isak," Tuva screeched, flung herself into her husband's arms and burst into tears.

"What is this now, my Tuva," Isak said, but she could tell he was just as choked up at their reunion.

They clung to each other for several moments before Isak pulled far enough away to hug his mother and father, then wrapped his arms around his wife again. He eventually pulled Tuva toward the kitchen table. He positioned two chairs close to each other so they could sit huddled together, reveling in their reunion.

The rest of the family gathered around the table, all talking at once, explaining how the last couple of months had gone for each of them. Tuva could tell Marriam was watching her and Isak, and her mother-in-law seemed pleased by the affection between them.

Isak periodically pulled Tuva into a hug or kiss until finally he said, "I don't think there has been a man in this world that has missed his wife as much as I have missed you, my Tuva."

"And you have no idea how much I have missed you, my Isak," Tuva said.

The front door burst open, and the family grew quiet. They all turned to see who was intruding on their private family reunion. Tuva noticed the instant Bill realized what was going on, and she exchanged a look with Marriam.

Isak stood, clinging to Tuva's hand, and said, "Bill, it's so good to see you. I can't thank you enough for taking such great care of my family."

Bill nodded once, but looked past Isak at Tuva. She looked up at her husband, hoping Bill could see how she felt about Isak. Isak looked down at Tuva with a questioning look before looking back at Bill.

"I suppose I will catch up in the morning. You should take this time with your family. See you tomorrow," Bill said.

"Thanks again. Have a good night. See you in the morning," Isak said.

Bill left, shutting the door behind him, and Isak turned back to Tuva.

He pulled her up to stand and kissed her gently. "We have so much to talk about. But for now, it is just wonderful having you in my arms again."

"It is indeed wonderful."

Chapter Seventeen

Tuva shut her trunk and secured it. She had just finished the final preparations for their trip up the coast to their new homestead. They would be leaving the following morning, and as excited as she was at the prospect of finally being in one place for good, she was also nervous about starting anew in a wilderness. The one thing giving her hope was knowing she would be with her husband, and she would still get to see the beautiful lake she had fallen in love with.

"Are you done, Tuva?" Isak hollered from the kitchen table.

Pushing the blanket wall aside, Tuva walked toward her husband. "All set. Now all we need to do is load it up in the morning."

"We have finalized our preparations too," Marriam said, while setting the table.

"Do you think we will be settled there before winter really hits hard?" Tuva asked.

"It will be tight, but I think we will make it in time," Isak said.

"Yes, our guide on the lake said they can usually still paddle along the water up until Christmas at times. Even though we already have snow, it doesn't always get too bad until after Christmas," Adam said.

"That is good to know," Tuva said. "Of course, with us going now, that gets us there and settled well before Christmas."

"I hope you like it there," Isak said. "We had to build small structures for now, but you and I will have a separate space for our bedroom with a covered porch in between the main cabin and our little room. In the winter, it won't be as convenient, but we will make do."

Heat rushed through Tuva at the thought of finally being alone with her husband.

Isak must have read her reaction, for he reached out to grab her hand. "I can't wait either."

The warmth in Tuva's cheeks rose, and she ducked her head, hoping Isak didn't notice. She rushed to go help Marriam with the final dinner preparations. Josef, Adam, and Wally walked in from outside just as Tuva placed the stew pot in the middle of the table.

"Just in time," Wally said, as he walked over to fill a bowl.

There were not enough chairs since Bill would be joining them, so some would sit by the fire, or on the floor while the rest sat at the table.

Bill walked in as Adam filled his bowl and said, "Smells good."

"Thank you," Marriam said. "It's a recipe I received from a friend after we moved to America. It has served me well on cold nights and limited provisions."

"Sounds like the perfect recipe to take with you on your journey," Bill said, sneaking glances at Tuva, which she pretended not to see.

Bill had tried talking to Tuva after Isak and his brothers returned, but Tuva quickly moved toward anyone close by. She refused to be alone with him, but wondered if she should have told him one last time that he would never have a chance with her.

Isak was saying something to her, and she pulled her thoughts from Bill and said, "I'm sorry, I didn't quite hear that."

"Where did you go?" Isak asked. "You were lost in thought somewhere."

She exchanged a look with Marriam. "Nowhere really, just thinking about the future."

"That is understandable," he said. "I was just asking you if you were excited about the boat ride tomorrow?"

"Well, if the boat doesn't roll over or throw a man overboard, it will be great," Tuva said.

Adam spit out the water he was drinking, coughed a few times, and started laughing. "Oh my, Tuva. You about choked me to death."

Everyone else chuckled except Bill, who had a confused expression on his face. Isak must have noticed his expression too, because he explained why Adam had responded the way he did.

Instead of joining in the glee, Bill looked over at Tuva. "That is quite the crossing. How traumatic that must have been for you."

She tried to hide her discomfort at Bill's tender response, and waved her hand in the air, saying, "It was fine. I'm fine."

Isak looked at her quizzically. She shrugged and shook her head, hoping it would dismiss any thoughts or questions he may have.

Isak looked over at Bill. "It is noble of you to be worried for my wife's care, but she is fine, Bill."

The room filled with tension as everyone grew quiet. Tuva steadily watched her husband and wondered if he knew about Bill's kiss. She adjusted her shoulders and decided to say something to defuse the situation.

She opened her mouth to speak, but Isak hooted and said, "Such a good friend, Bill. Thanks for watching out for my family. We will miss you."

Bill's countenance lightened, and he mumbled something about being happy to do it and dove into his food. He didn't say anything else the rest of the evening until he finished eating and left for the barn.

After Bill disappeared for the night, Wally asked, "What was that about?"

"What was what about?" Marriam asked.

"It was awkward in here for a minute, and I was having a hard time figuring out what was going on," Wally said.

Tuva looked over at Marriam but was relieved when she didn't see the same panic Tuva felt.

Marriam waved her hand dismissively. "That Bill is an odd one sometimes. Nice. But an odd one at times."

Wally seemed to take the explanation at face value, took his dishes to the kitchen, and prepared water for cleaning the dinner mess. Tuva loved how this family, her family, pitched in and helped. It was so different than the way things had been for her growing up.

Her smile faltered when she realized that Isak was watching her closely. She knew he would be asking her some questions later when they were alone, and she dreaded that conversation. But later never came. She wondered if he made up his own mind about things, or was too scared to ask. Either way, he never brought it up. When they went to bed, he just wrapped his arms around her and held her close until she fell asleep.

Tuva had a restless night of men chasing her and of drowning in the sea. She was thankful when the sun poked through the shutters, signaling a new day. Tuva threw her covers aside and stretched.

"Good morning," Isak said, rubbing Tuva's back. "Rough night?"

"How did you know?" she asked.

"You were thrashing about a couple of times."

"Oh. Well. Um. Yes. I was having a bad dream, but it's okay now."

"If you say so."

"I do," Tuva said, squeezing her husband's hand.

"Time to get up and around, you two," Josef hollered from the kitchen area.

They both chuckled and dove into getting ready for the day. Tuva could feel the sting of her nightmares fade as she prepared for her journey. Her excitement grew with each task until Isak started snickering.

"It is wonderful to see you so happy about today," Isak said, in between cackles.

"Stop making fun of me," Tuva said, wrapping her shawl around her shoulders. "Now, grab the last of our things and let's get a move on. Long day ahead."

"So, bossy too," Isak said. "I love it."

It was Tuva's turn to laugh as she followed her husband out to the waiting wagon and the rest of the family. Josef and Marriam were going to drive the wagon to the boat dock while the rest of them walked. Tuva glanced at the barn and wondered if Bill would be out to say goodbye, but she didn't see any movement.

She grabbed her husband's hand and squeezed it. "Let's go."

Isak pressed her hand in return. He looked over toward the barn, then back at Tuva with the same questioning look from the night before, and quickly replaced it with a smile. "I can't wait to start this next chapter with you."

"I can't wait either, my love," Tuva said.

A light jumped into Isak's eyes at the mention of the word love, and heat passed between them.

Isak leaned down and kissed Tuva. "Here's to our future."

The boat rounded a bend, heading into a small bay along the rugged coastline of the lake. Tuva could see a dock along a pebbled beach ahead. A structure was tucked in between some trees where a fresh clearing had been cut out of the vast forest. A sense of belonging washed over her.

This is home.

Tuva looked over at Isak who was looking at the same view. "It's beautiful, Isak."

Isak whipped his head around. "You love it?"

"I love it," she said. "This is the most beautiful place I have ever been to. I don't think I ever want to leave."

"This makes me so happy, my Tuva."

Marriam and Josef also stated their approval, but Tuva wondered at the worry resonating in Marriam's eyes.

When the boat reached the dock and everyone made their way to shore, Tuva pulled Marriam aside. "Are you okay?"

"So perceptive of you," Marriam said. "I will be fine. It's just so isolated, and I worry about us for the winter."

"I worry about that too, but together we can face anything," Tuva said. "I really believe that."

"I believe it too, so I will not let my fears detract from the excitement of the day," Marriam said.

"Good plan," Tuva said. "Now, let's get a closer look at our new home."

Tuva pushed the front door of the small cabin open and allowed her eyes to adjust to the dim room. The kitchen area was to the right, with two benches and two chairs surrounding a large table. A fireplace rested against the back wall, straight ahead, with two rocking chairs flanking each side. To the left was a small bedroom and a small water closet, which surprised Tuva.

"What is that?" she asked.

"We thought maybe it might be nice to use the bathroom inside the cabin instead of having to trudge through the snow in the winter," Isak said. "Me and my brothers will take turns emptying the slop bucket every day so the stench doesn't get so bad."

"What a brilliant idea," Tuva said.

"It was mine," Adam said, pointing at himself with pride.

Tuva chuckled and finished taking in her surroundings. A couple of screens made of wood and blankets blocked an area to the far left of the privy, and Tuva realized it was where Adam and Wally would sleep.

She remembered she and Isak would be sleeping in a detached bedroom, and Tuva walked toward the kitchen area. She found a side door leading to an outside covered porch. With Isak following behind, she rushed across to see her new bedroom.

Flinging the door open, Tuva sighed. It wasn't a big space, but it was going to be perfect for them. There was a fireplace in the corner, built-in shelves on one wall, and a small bed under a window on another wall.

"Well, what do you think?" Isak asked.

"It's perfect," Tuva said. "I can't wait to get settled."

"This is just for now, until we can build our own house," Isak said. But for the time being, I wanted us to have some privacy since we haven't had much of it since our wedding night."

Feeling panicked at being alone with Isak, Tuva tried to tamp down her fears of having a man touch her again. She wanted to make love to her husband, but the memory of her attack always seemed to snake in whenever her thoughts went in that direction.

"Are you okay?" Isak asked.

Forcing her fears aside, Tuva wrapped her fingers around the back of her husband's neck and slowly pulled him down to her mouth. She kissed him gently, but a spark was lit, and it grew more passionate.

Isak broke away. "Damn it, woman. I can't wait until we are really alone. If it wasn't for fear of one of my brothers marching in here at any moment, I would continue this dance between us."

Letting out a smug hoot, Tuva left the room to go help unload their things. It was time to get settled and start this new part of their life together.

Chapter Eighteen

Dear Nora,

We are finally settled into our new home tucked away in our own bay. The land Isak secured was far more than I thought, and I often wonder where my family got the wealth to do the things we are doing. I have never asked, and I don't ever intend to. I will just enjoy the benefits of living in the wilderness and starting our lives together.

I had forgotten how much furniture Isak and his brothers brought with them when they started our little homestead. And you would not believe the talent they have at making furniture and working with wood. Their creations are just beautiful. How are things with your new friend? Was a decision made about you getting married?

Christmas has come and gone, and we are all snowed in here. I'm not sure if I will be able to send this letter until spring, so you may receive several at once.

The winter has been harsh at times. We have had several terrible storms where the wind howled, and the waves of the great lake crashed. But when the storms passed, the beauty was always breathtaking.

I miss you terribly.

Give Mamma and Pappa all my love.

Tuva

Chapter Nineteen

Large snowflakes fell gracefully outside the kitchen window. Tuva stood at the washbasin cleaning the last of the lunch mess. She was watching Isak chop wood, and her thoughts kept straying to their night in bed. Her cheeks flamed, and she pressed her hand to her forehead as though to cool the heat radiating from her memories.

Their first night back together had been a good one, but there were many times Tuva had to work through feelings of fear while being intimate. She often struggled to overcome thoughts of her attack when she went to bed at night, alone with her husband.

Isak would ask if it was him, but she would either indicate she was out of practice or tired from the day's activities. Thankfully, Isak never pressed and eventually she was able to work through her fears and the passion between them grew.

Tuva now spent a lot of time in the evenings getting to know her husband again and she was enjoying every minute of it. A frown crossed her lips as Tuva realized Isak had still not said he loved her. She hadn't either, but she was afraid to say it first.

"You okay?" Marriam asked from behind her.

"Yes," Tuva said while she finished tidying the kitchen. "I was just thinking."

"Are you and Isak okay?"

Tuva couldn't stop the rush of blood in her cheeks as she said, "Oh, we are just fine."

Marriam chuckled. "Glad to hear."

"I still wonder sometimes how he really feels about me ..." Tuva's words trailed off before she pointed out the window. "Do you see that?"

Marriam rushed to see what Tuva was pointing at. "Oh, it looks like people."

Tuva threw on her coat and wrapped a shawl around her arms before running outside.

She had just met up with Isak when recognition set in. She hollered, "Minwaadizi."

Tuva started to run toward the Ojibwe when Isak reached out to grab her arm. "Wait a minute. We need to be careful."

"Don't be ridiculous," Tuva said. "They are wonderful people."

Isak let go of her arm, and she ran toward her friend. Minwaadizi broke away from her family and they embraced with glee. Makwa said something Tuva couldn't understand.

Minwaadizi paused, looked over her shoulder at her husband, and said, "My friend, Tuva."

Realization flooded across Makwa's face as he studied Tuva, and he said hello.

Tuva returned the greeting before turning back to Minwaadizi. "You were right. I was reunited with my Isak."

"I knew you would be."

Tuva hugged her again. "Come, meet my husband, and then you must warm yourself by our fire."

"We are okay to stay out here," Makwa said.

"Nonsense, it is freezing. Please, my gift to you for all that you have done for me."

The corner of Makwa's lips lifted slightly. He said something in his dialect and followed Tuva toward the house. When she met up with Isak, introductions were made, and they went into the house. Marriam and Josef called out greetings, and everyone gathered around the fireplace.

"How did you meet Tuva?" Isak asked.

Makwa started to answer, but Tuva interrupted. "We met on the road, and again at the market."

Minwaadizi studied her, before whispering, "He does not know."

"No, and I want to keep it that way, if possible."

"Secrets are never good, my friend," Minwaadizi said.

"You're probably right, but I don't know how to share this secret," Tuva said.

"We will respect your decision on this," Minwaadizi said.

The conversation in the room changed to the weather and the harshness of winter along the lake, until Tuva asked, "What brings you to our home?"

"We used to live on these lands, but now we only travel through them," Makwa said. "When we heard that someone new was living here, we wanted to see. We heard he was a kind and fair man."

"I hope to always be regarded as a kind and fair man," Isak said.

"How long will you be staying?" Tuva asked.

"We are just passing," Minwaadizi said. "We will meet with a small group of our people a few days walk from here."

"Does this mean you will be living in this area?" Tuva asked.

"No," Minwaadizi said. "We will stay until spring, but we keep moving."

"I will miss you," Tuva said.

"And I you," Minwaadizi said.

"Would you care to stay for dinner, or stay the night?" Tuva asked.

"This is a kind offer," Makwa said. "But we must return to our camp."

A silence fell over the room before Isak started to ask another question, but Makwa interrupted him. "We come with a warning."

Tuva started to panic. Had they unintentionally done something to ancient Ojibwe land? Were they going to be told they needed to leave and never return?

"Copper will not be found here," Makwa said.

"What?" Isak asked. "How do you know?"

"I grew up on this land. Walked this land. Fished these waters. There is no copper found here," Makwa said.

Tuva knew the color drained from her cheeks.

She looked over at Minwaadizi, who said, "It is true, my friend."

"But we poured our whole lives into coming here for that purpose," Tuva said.

"What we think is our purpose, isn't always our real purpose," Minwaadizi said. "If you respect this land. If you respect gichi-gami. You may prosper."

"Gichi-gami will be deadly, but she will provide you life. Take care of her," Makwa said.

"What is gichi-gami?" Isak asked.

"In words you understand, it means great water, big sea."

Chapter Twenty

Dear Nora,

Spring is finally here again. The nights are still cool and the wind off the lake makes it feel colder than what it is, I think. But we see buds on the trees and flowers poking out of the ground. Marriam and I have picked a small place for a garden and are excited to get that going as soon as the ground is workable.

Isak and his brothers say they have found where they think will be a good place to start their copper mine. I fear for them in this venture based on some information given to us by some friends a few months ago. Whatever happens, though, we will remain.

Give Mamma and Pappa my love,

Tuva

Chapter Twenty-One

Marriam finished the last row of planting just as Tuva brought the last bucket of water. They had spent most of the day in the garden, and Tuva was pleased with the work they accomplished. It wouldn't be a big garden this year because they wanted to experiment to find out what would grow in this harsher climate.

Tuva had asked for some advice from Minwaadizi, and based on her input, they created the garden before them. Tuva watered the dirt until the bucket was empty. She put it on the ground at her feet and stretched her arms in the air, hoping to relieve the pain in her shoulders and back.

"A warm bath will do us both good," Marriam said as she gathered her garden tools.

"Yes, it will, but first, I will start preparing dinner. Our men should be coming soon."

"I hope today was more successful for them," Marriam said while she walked beside Tuva toward the cabin.

"I do too," Tuva said. She lifted her hand to cover her eyes and squinted. "Is that a boat that just rounded the point?"

Marriam looked in the direction Tuva described. "I believe it is. Maybe it's someone who is feeling sorry for us, and bringing us supplies."

Tuva laughed and walked down to the dock to wait. She noticed Marriam went to take care of the garden tools, but was sure she would join her eventually. As the boat approached the edge of the dock, Tuva realized instantly who it was.

"Why, Bill. This is a surprise," Tuva said, not sure how to feel about his sudden visit.

"It's good to see you, Tuva," Bill said. He jumped onto the dock while another man secured the boat. "This is my friend Joshua Culver."

"Oh, I have heard of you," Tuva said. "You are the one that created Duluth, right?"

"Something like that," Joshua said.

"Welcome to our home," Tuva said, sticking out her hand. "I'm Tuva Nilsson, and that is my mother-in-law Marriam Nilsson walking toward us."

"It is an honor to meet you both," Joshua said. "Is your husband about?"

"They will be returning any moment, Mr. Culver," Marriam said.

As if on cue, Josef appeared from a small path in the trees with Wally following close behind. Tuva could tell when he realized they had guests because he brushed his clothes off and wiped his hands on a rag he had in his back pocket. Wally didn't do anything to straighten his appearance, but his constant grin widened.

"Josef," Marriam called out, "come meet our guest, Joshua Culver, and of course you remember Bill."

"Having visitors is a surprise," Josef said.

"Come on up to the house," Tuva said. "Bring your things. It will be too late for you to return to Duluth tonight."

"Thank you for your hospitality, Mrs. Nilsson," Joshua said.

Bill nodded but didn't say anything as he passed by Tuva to gather his things. Tuva offered her assistance, but the men turned her down.

"Always so kind," Bill said.

"I try to be," Tuva said. Her cheeks grew warm, and she looked down at the ground to avoid looking at Bill any longer.

"Please, let us know where we should bring our things," Joshua said as he neared Tuva.

Tuva only nodded and led the way up to the cabin. Once they reached the porch, Wally and Josef offered their assistance, and they all went inside. Marriam directed the men where to leave their things and Tuva went to wash up and start dinner. She was just finishing peeling the potatoes when Isak walked in with Adam on his heels. His concerned look quickly vanished when he noticed Bill.

Bill crossed the room with his outstretched hand toward Isak. "It is so great to see you, my friend."

"Wonderful to see you too, Bill," Isak said. "And Joshua Culver, what are you doing all the way up here?"

"You know each other?" Tuva asked.

"Yes. Bill introduced me before I set out to ready our homestead. We had a great evening of sharing our hopes for the future, and drinking plenty of beer."

"Oh, that was the night you came home reeking of a pub and passed out on our bed," Tuva said.

"That would be the night," Isak said with a sheepish look.

"In answer to your question, Bill and I decided to come up and make sure you made it through the winter. We brought some supplies we thought you might need, as well," Joshua said.

"That is mighty generous of you," Isak said. "Just let me know how much I owe you for them."

"We can figure that out later," Bill said.

"Please, make yourself at home," Isak said. "I'm going to go get cleaned up for dinner."

Isak's brothers and father followed his lead and excused themselves to also get cleaned up. Marriam mumbled something about needing to talk with Josef about something, and Tuva found herself alone with Bill and Joshua. Joshua made himself comfortable by the fireplace, while Bill walked over to the kitchen area and leaned against the tiny counter.

Tuva's hands faltered under his scrutiny, and she tried to ignore the awkward tension.

"We should talk," Bill whispered.

"We have nothing to talk about, Bill," Tuva said quietly. "I don't understand why you would think that we do."

"Perhaps I'm mistaken, but you looked glad to see me," Bill said, "and I saw you looking over at the barn the day you left."

"I looked at the barn because I was surprised you didn't come out to say goodbye to your friends," Tuva said.

"Are you discussing life's greatest problems?" Joshua asked. "Your tone sounds serious, even though I can't quite make out what you're saying."

"Nonsense," Bill said, "We are just discussing the weather, and how wonderful of a homestead they have here."

"Oh, then I must join you," Joshua said, making his way toward the kitchen area.

"We will finish this later, Tuva," Bill whispered, and turned to Joshua. "The Nilssons make things with such fine craftsmanship, don't they?"

"They do indeed," Joshua said, studying Tuva too closely for her comfort. She was worried he heard some of what Bill had said, and she wondered if he knew what had happened between her and Bill.

Marriam entered the room and walked over to assist Tuva with preparing dinner. The men went to stand by the fireplace.

She glanced at Bill, then leaned toward Tuva, and whispered, "You okay?"

"I'm okay. This is just unnerving for me," Tuva said. "I wonder if I should have shared with Isak what happened. But I'm also fearful that if he finds out, things will fall apart for us, just as things are starting to come together."

"I will support you, no matter what you decide to do, my dear," Marriam reassured.

"I just don't want to hurt him."

"You won't."

Isak opened the door with a loud greeting, and Tuva changed the subject. Tuva could feel Isak studying her before he walked over to chat with their guests. She worried he may have heard some of what was said, but attempted to push it out of her mind while she finished preparing the meal.

Plates were filled, conversations ensued, and dinner was a success, even though everyone was scattered about the small room. Tuva made sure to stay close to Isak. Bill had always questioned her when she would profess her feelings for Isak, and she was impatient with him. She wondered yet again if she had somehow led him on in allowing his visits after her attack.

Isak reached over and squeezed her hand, and whispered, "Are you okay? You are so quiet this evening."

"Just a long day," she said.

"The garden looks really good. You did a great job," Isak said.

"Thank you. It was fun working with your mamma," Tuva said.

"Are you talking about the garden?" Marriam asked.

"I was just telling Tuva that it looks great," Isak said. "You both did a great job."

"As much as I know a garden, Tuva adds a wealth of knowledge, and I learned a few things," Marriam said with a wink at Tuva.

The heat in Tuva's cheeks grew and her countenance brightened for the first time that evening. She looked across the room at her mother-in-law and beamed.

"This dinner has been real fine too," Joshua interjected.

"Tuva is a great cook," Wally said, while gathering plates and dishes to take to the kitchen area.

"Wally, I will get the dishes," Tuva said. "You should go with the men outside."

"That is our cue, gentlemen," Isak said. "Shall we head outside and discuss the real reason why you decided to head our way?"

Isak led the men outside while Tuva dove into cleaning up the dinner mess. The cabin became quiet after the door closed, and she was sure Marriam was watching her again while she scrubbed the plates.

Unable to bear the silence any longer, Tuva said, "I'm fine, Marriam. I promise I am. Having the praise of my husband, and from the rest of the family, lightened my mood. If he decides to try and talk with me again, I will lay it out for him once and for all."

"I think you have already done that on more than one occasion," Marriam said. "If he pushes, then let me know, and I will step in to help."

"Thank you, but I think I can handle it."

"Handle what?" Wally asked.

The pot Tuva held slipped through her fingers and clanked at the bottom of the water basin. "Honestly, Wally, you startled me," Tuva said.

"Sorry about that, sis," Wally said. "Can I ask though ... is someone giving you a hard time? Because if that is the case, I can take care of it."

"Nonsense," Marriam said. "And what have I taught you about listening to other people's conversations?"

"Sorry, Mamma," Wally said.

"That's okay," Marriam said with a wave of her hand. "What are you doing back in here, anyway?"

"Pappa sent me in to gather some mugs. Bill brought some beer from town."

"I see," Mamma said. "Gather them and get on with yourself."

Wally nodded, gathered the mugs, hugged Tuva, then Marriam, and went back outside to the hum of male voices mixed with laughter. The same murmurs continued through the evening as the sun began to sink lower, bringing the darkness of the night close behind.

Tuva decided to go to bed as she couldn't keep her eyes open any longer. She called a goodnight to the men as she crossed the connecting porch to her and

Isak's bedroom. Isak mumbled something about being along shortly, but she knew it would probably be a late night for him.

Isak eventually crawled into bed next to her, awakening her from her troubled slumber. He kissed her on the cheek and then passed out on his pillow, leaving Tuva to lie awake for several hours contemplating what she was going to tell Isak about the situation with Bill. A faint line of pink shone in the distance, signaling a new day before Tuva fell back to sleep.

Chapter Twenty-Two

Water sloshed over the rim of the bucket and splashed the hem of Tuva's dress. She readjusted the bucket and continued her ascent toward the cabin. She had risen long before anyone else and decided to get coffee and breakfast started.

Tuva walked into the kitchen. At the sight of Bill standing there, the cool liquid slipped over the rim a second time as she fumbled with the handle, trying not to drop it.

"Bill, you startled me," Tuva hissed, gathering her composure while walking toward the counter.

"Sorry about that," Bill said. "I was just hoping to get a chance to talk with you before everyone else woke up."

"We will not be discussing anything in here," Tuva whispered.

"So, you agree we need to discuss this. Us."

"That is not what I said. And there is no us ... never has been."

Tuva started to prepare the coffee and set out some items to begin the breakfast preparations. Her nerves became more unraveled the longer Bill stood watching her move about.

Finally, she slammed a towel on the counter. "Have it your way. Let's go discuss this by the water."

Bill's shoulders relaxed and a smile spread across his face.

"Don't think for a moment that this gives you any hope," Tuva said.

Tuva led the way down toward the dock and watched the sun change the color of the water. She took a deep breath of the cool air, closed her eyes, and some of the tension eased from her body.

"This view always renews me," she whispered.

"You look absolutely beautiful in the morning sun, Tuva," Bill said.

"You can't talk like that with me," she said. "I have said this before, Bill. I'm sorry if my actions led you on after my attack. You must know that I was just grasping at any kind of friendship and comfort during that time. It meant nothing. Please don't make me regret our friendship because you were there for me during my darkest moments."

Bill reached across the distance and gingerly grabbed her hand.

Tuva tried to pull it away, but he held tight. "No, wait. Please, Tuva."

She hesitated while Bill took a deep breath, and said, "Look, I know that I will probably never have a chance with you. And my heart aches knowing this. I just need to know that you are cared for."

He paused and let go of her hand, but stepped closer to her.

"Tuva, if you could have seen what I saw when Makwa brought you to me that day. You were so battered, and bruised, and broken, and my heart just fell apart for you. I felt compelled to put you back together. And in that process, I fell in love with you. I know Isak has never said those words to you."

"How do you know that?" Tuva asked.

"Because I see the longing in your eyes, waiting for him to do so," Bill said. "It's the same longing I have for you."

"Please, you must stop talking to me like this," Tuva said.

"I need to have my say, and then I will stop, I promise," Bill said. "I'm not trying to give you a hard time or make things difficult, but our conversations have always been short or cut off and I want us to have some peace between us."

Tuva walked to the edge of the dock and wrapped her arms around herself.

Bill didn't follow, but he continued his speech. "I know I don't have the right to say these things to you. I also know I'm dishonoring my friendship with your husband. But I've had time to think on this and believe if I don't do this I will forever wonder. If you tell me now that I will never have a chance with you. That you love him. That he loves you. I will stay silent going forward and continue with my life, knowing you are happy."

Moisture built in her eyes, spilling over into gentle streams down her cheeks. She wished she could tell Bill that Isak had professed his love for her, but he hadn't. He had shown affection and care for her but never said the words, but she reminded herself, neither had she.

Bill's hand rested on her shoulder, and she turned toward him while he pulled her into a gentle hug. Tuva knew she should pull away, knowing he wouldn't understand why she needed comfort, but found she couldn't.

Instead, she said, "Bill, you must understand. Although my husband and I have never expressed our love for one another in words, I'm devoted to him, and I will always be devoted to him. You and I can never be and will never be."

"Do you have love for me too?" he asked.

"I know that you wish I could say that I love you in the way you want to be loved, but I do not care for you in that way," Tuva said. "You were a bright light for me during my darkest days. You encouraged me to not give up on life. You gave me a reason to get up every day. And for that, I will always be grateful. And in a small part of my heart, I will always have a love for you that I do not have for others. But it isn't the same kind of care or love that you want or need from a companion in life."

Bill hugged her closer, kissed the top of her head, and let go. He took a step back, started to speak again, but was cut off.

"What is going on?"

Tuva's entire world crashed around her feet as she swung around. "Isak. Isak, it's not what you might think."

"No," Isak said. "I wondered if something was going on with you two when I came to get you last fall. I refused to believe it though. But now I know I was right."

"Isak, we should explain," Bill said.

"Do you love my wife?" Isak asked.

Bill's shoulders slumped forward. "Yes."

Isak took two steps forward and punched Bill in the face, knocking him into Tuva. She stumbled back, tried to keep from falling into the water, and landed hard against the dock boards. Isak rushed forward and bent over her.

Isak pulled Tuva to her feet and asked, "Are you okay? I didn't mean to knock you over."

"I'm fine," she said, while her lips trembled. Their eyes locked, and she whispered, "I don't love him."

Isak released her and stomped toward the cabin.

"Isak, you must listen, please," Tuva cried out.

"She's right, Isak. It's not her fault," Bill said.

Isak didn't slow his pace, and Tuva rushed after him.

"Isak, please," she cried.

"I was just trying to be a good friend after her attack," Bill called.

Tuva froze, the blood seeping out of her cheeks. She swung around to Bill, shaking her head, mouthing, no.

"What attack?" Isak asked.

"You didn't tell him?" Bill asked.

Tuva's shoulders slumped forward and she looked away.

"Oh, Tuva," Bill said.

"What a mess I've made," Tuva said. She forced herself to take big breaths to keep from falling apart. She wanted to bury her face and sob, but knew she had to try to keep her composure.

"What attack?" Isak asked again.

Tuva looked over at her husband and could tell his anger had changed to concern.

She must have looked a wreck, because he rushed to her side, but stopped short of folding her into his arms. "Tuva, what is it?"

Giving in, Tuva covered her face with her hands and collapsed in a heap of sobs.

"Would someone please tell me what is going on?" Isak yelled.

"Isak, I think we all need some time to cool off, and then we will discuss this again," Marriam said from behind.

Isak turned toward his mother and asked, "Do you know?"

"Yes, my son. And I promise you, it is not what you think," Marriam said.

Tuva watched her husband's every move through her tears. When he looked down on her, she shrank back at the pain she read in his eyes. She held out a hand to his, and he helped her up, but instead of holding her, which is what she needed, he stomped off toward the trail behind the house.

"Isak, wait. Please," Tuva hollered, but he never slowed. She could only watch him disappear into the forest.

"Let him go, my dear," Marriam said.

"What have I done?" Tuva said, and crumbled into Marriam's arms.

"Bill, can you fetch some more water please, and help Josef in the kitchen," Marriam said.

"Yes, I can do that," Bill said.

Marriam mumbled a thank you and helped Tuva to her room. When the door was closed behind them, Marriam helped Tuva to the bed, still crumpled from the night's sleep. Tuva sat on the edge of the bed, took some long deep breaths, and forced herself to gain control.

"What happened this morning, Tuva?" Marriam asked.

"I woke up early after a restless night, and found Bill waiting for me in the kitchen," Tuva said. "I told him we shouldn't talk in the house. I didn't want to wake anyone, and I knew we needed to be able to speak freely. So, we went to the dock. He said some things. I told him how I felt. He hugged me. I let him. Which was probably a mistake, but it was like a good-bye for me to a friendship that I desperately needed for a time. And then Isak stumbled on us. I have no idea what he heard, and then you saw and heard the rest."

Marriam patted Tuva's hand. "This is partly my fault. I told you it was okay to keep this a secret."

"I should have known better though," Tuva said. "I know that secrets and lies never get anyone anywhere."

"You haven't been lying, Tuva."

"Maybe, but I haven't told my husband what happened either."

A knock at the door interrupted Marriam before she could respond to Tuva. Instead, she said, "Yes, who is it?"

"It's me, Mamma," Wally said. "I thought Tuva could use a warm washcloth and a cup of coffee."

"Come in, my boy," Marriam said with tenderness.

Wally walked in and placed the warm bowl of water and rag on the dresser, and took the coffee to Tuva. He placed the mug in her hands and wrapped his fingers around hers. "I know you love my brother, Tuva. And I know whatever this misunderstanding is, will be fixed. And I'm also sorry to know that you have been carrying a heavy burden alone."

"Wally, you have such a gentle heart," Tuva said, smiling through her tears.

He kneeled before her and asked, "Are you okay, sister?"

She took a sip of her coffee while Marriam prepared a warm compress.

"I will be," Tuva whispered, cradling the mug.

"My brother is an idiot."

"Oh goodness," Tuva said. "He is not an idiot."

"He has never told you how he feels. Idiot."

Tuva chuckled. Wally and Marriam joined her.

"This is not funny," Tuva said in between giggles.

"Perhaps not, but it's good to hear you laugh instead of cry," Marriam said.

"You, my dear friends," Tuva said.

"You mean us, your family," Wally corrected.

"Yes. My family," Tuva agreed. "I love you all so much."

"Including Isak," Wally said. "I know you do. I watch the two of you together. It's so evident."

"I often wonder how he feels, and I often believe he loves me. I just don't know why he has never said the words," Tuva said.

"Perhaps it's fear that keeps him from saying it," Marriam said.

There was a commotion outside, and Wally went to the window.

"Looks like Joshua and Bill are loading their boat," he said over his shoulder.

Tuva took her coffee over to the dresser. She dipped the now chilled cloth into the warm water, squeezed, and placed it against her face. She breathed in the scent of lemon soap as she slowly washed away the tears. She cleansed her face a few more times before turning to say with a confidence she didn't feel,

"We should go break our fast and then face whatever comes next."

Chapter Twenty-Three

The heat from the sun soaked into Tuva's skin as she sat on the dock with her face lifted to the sky. She could hear Bill and Joshua talking with Josef by the porch about final arrangements between the Nilssons and Joshua. They had agreed on a contract to allow Joshua to log a few acres of their land, plus the Nilssons would be selling furniture in the general store Joshua was starting soon. In return, Joshua would have goods delivered once a month until the harshest parts of winter set in.

It was a good agreement for both families, and Tuva was glad her debacle with Bill hadn't ruined it. Hearing someone approach, Tuva turned just as Bill stepped onto the dock.

Tuva started to profess her discouragement in having him be there, but he held up his hand and said, "I know. Probably not the best timing, but if Isak doesn't return soon, Joshua and I will need to head out, if we are to make it back to Duluth again before nightfall. And I don't know when I will see you again."

"Fair enough," she said.

Bill moved closer, but instead of sitting next to her, he sat and leaned against a piling a few feet away from her. Tuva turned toward him as he started talking.

"I'm so sorry about saying something about your attack," Bill said. "I had no idea that you hadn't shared that with him yet. Which makes me wonder about you two."

"Stop using any lack of communication on my part, or my husband's part, as a sense of hope for you," Tuva said. "I know I don't profess how I feel for my husband, but it is hard for me to share those things with someone else when I haven't shared them with him yet."

Tuva paused and looked out toward the blue of her lake. "Our marriage, like most, started with very little knowledge about each other, and although we cared for one another on our wedding day, I know our feelings have grown. At least mine have. Especially on this journey we have had. He will always be my one and only, Bill. And I just pray we can work past this mountain that is between us."

"He would be a foolish man not to try and figure this out with you," Bill said. "I'm sorry for my part in causing you pain, and for causing you friction with Isak."

"Thank you for that."

"I think I will always love you, Tuva," he said. "But I know that it will never be for us. Just know you will always have a friend in me. If you should ever need anything. And I mean, anything, don't hesitate to ask it of me."

"You are a sweet man," Tuva said. "I will always be thankful for the friendship we had. I especially needed it at that time."

"How are you doing with all of that now?" he asked.

Tuva stared past him. Speaking in monotone, she said, "I still occasionally have nightmares. I sometimes have flashbacks, especially when I go for walks alone and it's starting to get dark out. I know we are secluded out here, but I still sometimes feel like I have eyes watching me, even though I know no one is there. I also have times I can't get clean enough, especially after one of my nightmares."

"I wish that day had never happened," Bill said.

"Me too," Tuva agreed. "I'm sorry for any part I played in this mess."

"You did nothing wrong, Tuva," Bill said. "At least with me."

"Maybe, but I did hurt Isak," Tuva said. "And I will always regret that."

Tuva caught movement over by the trail leading into the forest. She stood, hoping it would be Isak. Her lips curved up, but her heart started pounding as nerves coursed through her. She looked down at Bill, and he turned in Isak's direction.

Isak paused when he looked toward the dock, and Tuva knew the second he realized she was with Bill ... again. His guarded expression fell, but was quickly replaced with anger. He turned to head back into the trees when Wally came out of nowhere, stopping him.

Tuva couldn't hear the whole conversation, but she did hear snippets of Wally telling Isak he was being a fool. Bill stood as she rushed past him.

"Tuva," Bill said, stopping her. She turned toward him one last time and he continued. "Remember, I'm always here. No matter what. And I will always love you."

"Thank you, my friend," Tuva said, and hurried toward the cabin.

Marriam came out onto the porch as Tuva got closer, and she held out her hand. When Tuva grabbed it, Marriam asked, "Everything finally settled?"

"Yes," Tuva said. "Now, time to have a talk with Isak."

"We do need to talk," Isak said from behind.

Tuva turned in his direction and noticed Bill moving to stand next to Isak, keeping a few feet between them. An awkward silence fell over the group, and she thought her heart would pound out of her chest. She looked from Isak to Bill and back to Isak, waiting for someone to say something.

"If no one else is going to speak, I will," Wally said, as he settled in on the other side of Tuva.

Tuva's lips curled slightly, and she looked down at her feet to hide her smile at Wally's protection of her. Leave it to him to lighten, or at least try to lighten the mood. She forced the grin away and looked up, locking eyes with Isak. She could tell he was holding back the same smile.

"Isak," she finally said, "Hurting you was the last thing any of us wanted to do. But it was the thing that was done, and I'm truly so very sorry for that."

Isak stared at her, and she struggled to read his guarded expression, before he said, "I'm not sure if I'm ready to hear what happened, but I know I can't wait another moment to have an explanation."

"Alright then," Marriam said. "Let's get settled because this is going to be a hard conversation, son."

"Tuva didn't do anything wrong," Bill interjected. "You need to know that."

"You don't love Bill?" Isak asked, looking only at Tuva.

"Of course not," Tuva said.

"Did he find a way into your bed?" Isak asked.

"Isak, of all the things to ask in front of all of us," Marriam said.

"It's a fair question," Tuva said, never breaking eye contact with Isak. "The answer is no."

"Then why is there such an intimacy between you?" Isak asked. "I can feel it."

"It isn't an intimacy like you think. At least not on my part," Tuva said.

"I will be honest," Bill interjected. "I do love your wife, Isak. I wish I didn't, but the time we spent together. Well, I just fell in love with her."

"Easy to do," Isak whispered.

Tuva softened at her husband's comment, and she desperately wanted to leap into his arms, but instead she guarded herself, because she knew all the cards were about to be laid on the table.

"I kissed her," Bill said. "And she pushed me away."

Something flared in Isak's eyes before he glared at Bill. "Now I don't feel sorry for punching you."

"You had every right to do that," Bill said. "I conjured things in my head from our time together that I thought were there, but I was wrong."

"And there never would be anything either," Tuva said.

Isak looked over at Tuva, then to his mother, and asked, "You knew about all of this?"

"Isak, I thought it best to not say anything, for fear of what it might lead to," Marriam said. "It was purely out of a protection for you."

"But why would he have been spending so much time with Tuva?" Isak asked.

A flush of pain charged through Tuva's body as the reason for the time spent with Bill raced through her mind. She placed a hand on her stomach and felt like she was going to be sick. The blood drained from her face, and she locked eyes with Isak.

Will he think less of me? Will he never want to touch me again?

"What is it?" Isak asked.

"I think I need to sit down," she said, swaying on her feet. Marriam and Wally grabbed her arms to keep her from collapsing, and Isak stepped forward.

"You're scaring me," Isak said. "What happened?"

Tuva sat in the closest rocking chair and leaned her head back, closing her eyes. The attack played over and over in her mind, while fresh tears rained down her cheeks. A hand cradled hers and she snatched it away before realizing it was Marriam's.

"Only if you are ready, and able, my dear," Marriam said.

"Mamma, what happened to her?" Isak asked. "You mentioned an attack, Bill. What attack? Would some-one please just tell me?"

"Only if, or when, she is ready, friend. It's no one else's story to tell," Bill said.

"Wally, do you know what happened?" Isak asked.

"I know as much as you," Wally said. "But I know Tuva. I can see that this is bringing her great pain. Don't you see it too?"

"I do. Which is why I need to know," Isak said.

Tuva straightened her spine, sitting upright in her chair. She looked over at Bill. "I don't know if I can share it."

"What can I do?" Bill asked, stepping closer to the porch.

"Perhaps start with Makwa," Tuva said.

"Makwa? What does Makwa have to do with this?" Isak asked. Confusion flitted across his face before he said, "That day, when they were here. He started to say something, but you cut him off, Tuva. Does everyone on the lake know but me?"

"No," Tuva said. "At least I hope not."

"Son, perhaps you should take a seat," Josef said.

Tuva hadn't even realized he was there and jumped at his voice.

Isak sat on the front steps and looked out toward the water, then to Bill.

Bill glanced at Tuva, and she nodded.

"You hadn't been gone long when one night at dusk Makwa showed up at my door," Bill started. He was with his wife and family, and Tuva. All he shared with me was that they happened upon Tuva being attacked."

"What do you mean, attacked?" Isak asked.

"I will let her share those details," Bill said. "That was the first time I met her. She was badly, um, injured."

"The man was trying to rape me," Tuva blurted out.

Wally jumped to his feet. Marriam and Josef exchanged a look. Joshua and Adam mumbled curses. The color drained from Isak's face and Bill looked over at Tuva with such tenderness, Tuva almost regretted that she didn't love him in return. Almost.

Isak stood slowly, walked over to his wife, and knelt at her feet. He cradled her hands in his. Tuva's heart was racing, and she wondered if this would be the last of any intimacy between them.

"Oh, my dear wife," Isak said with such pain in his voice, it made Tuva weep even more. "I don't even know what to say."

"I don't either," Tuva said. "I was so scared to tell you. I was afraid you would reject me. I was afraid you would think I was damaged."

Isak glanced at his mother. "How bad was it?"

"It was bad," Marriam said. "She was battered and bruised, with scratches and gashes on her legs and arms. Her dress was ripped to shreds. And her face, oh it was heart-wrenching to see it."

Tuva locked eyes with Isak and tried to read his expression. He didn't say anything else.

He studied her before turning to Bill. "Thank you for watching out for her. What happened to the man who did this?"

"Um, I can answer that question," Joshua jumped in. "I must say, I didn't realize that your wife was the woman he attacked. I'm sorry for that. He escaped a couple of weeks after your wife's, um, incident. He ended up breaking into a house where he was shot and killed by the owner."

Tuva started trembling and hot tears rained down her cheeks. The comfort of her bed called to her.

Will these waves of emotions ever end?

Isak's thumb skimmed the back of her hand. She wished he would say something else, anything, because his silence made her fears feel more validated. She worried he would never want to be intimate with her again and as much as she tried to squash those fears, his silence seemed to confirm it.

Tuva gathered all her strength and stood. Isak let go of her hand and took a step back. A wave of shame washed over her, and she swayed on her feet. Bill took a step forward, as did Wally, but Tuva steadied herself as she looked out at her gichi-gami.

"I think I'm going to go lay down for a bit," she said. "Bill, Joshua, as much as I know you would like to return to Duluth today, I do believe it's getting too late in the day. Perhaps you should think on staying one more night."

Tuva forced herself to move. She walked to her room, shutting the door behind her. She had no idea what was said after she left or what was decided, and she didn't care. She laid down on her bed and allowed sleep to take over.

Chapter Twenty-Four

Tuva woke with a start. She rolled over, her brain in a fog. She concentrated on the ceiling until it came into focus before sitting up. She slid her hand toward her husband's side of the bed, but found the space bare. She scanned the room and discovered he was lying on the floor with a quilt over him. Her heart fell.

Will we ever be able to get past this?

Trying not to wake her husband, Tuva quickly dressed, grabbed her shawl, and went out to greet the morning sun by the water. She had her eyes closed, but knew she wasn't alone by the footsteps quietly approaching behind her.

"You doing okay?" Adam asked.

Tuva pulled her shawl tighter. "I have had better days."

"I'm so sorry for what happened, Tuva."

"Thank you, brother."

"You know, we have been through a lot the past couple of years," Adam said. "That boat ride over, the fire, all of it. You persevered through all of it with a strength and resilience that most can only admire in another."

"That is kind of you to say, but I don't feel very strong right now."

"But you are," Adam said. "You never let anything beat you. Don't let this beat you, either. He just needs time."

"Yes, I would imagine he does."

"He loves you, you know," he said softly.

"Does he?" Tuva questioned with a whisper.

"He has a hard time saying it for some reason, but I know he does. Everything he has done and will do is all for you."

"Well, everything I have done and will do is all for him."

"Maybe you should take some time to heal," Adam said. "You both need the time to heal, then you will be able to come together stronger for it."

"When did you get so wise?" Tuva asked with a laugh.

"I learned it from my big sister," Adam said tenderly.

"Adam, where is that water?" Marriam hollered from the porch.

"Just coming, Mamma," he said. He picked up the bucket at his feet. "I better get the water inside. You know Mamma."

"That I do," Tuva said.

She watched Adam fill the bucket and head to the cabin. Tuva turned back to her view, breathed in the moist air, and gazed at the mix of pinks and oranges reflecting on the small ripples splashing against the shore. She soaked in the beauty until the ache in her heart eased just enough.

Thinking it was best to tackle the day, she headed toward the kitchen. Tuva caught Isak in their bedroom window, watching her, and decided to go face him instead. When she walked in, he was sitting on the made bed fully dressed, with no signs he had slept on the floor the night before.

Tuva gathered her courage and asked, "Are you okay?"

"I want to be," he said.

"I want to be too," she said.

"Now that we are alone, Tuva, please tell me one more time ... what happened with Bill?" Isak asked.

"You already know that story."

"But I need to hear it without an audience."

"Bill was a friend to me after I got attacked. I needed a distraction, friendship, something to help me through. It was never inappropriate until it was. And when it was, I stopped it immediately. When you returned, I reinforced how I felt about him and you."

"That day we left, you looked at the barn right before leaving. Why?"

"I was surprised he didn't come out to say goodbye to you. But I was relieved I didn't have to deal with him."

"What about yesterday as he held you? You let him do that," he said.

"I did, but not for the reason you think. Bill was a good friend to me. Even though he was an idiot. I was saying goodbye to the friendship we once had, because things will never be the same between us."

"I'm glad he was there for you."

"He was there when I needed someone the most."

"That should have been me."

"But you couldn't be, and that's okay."

"You're right that I couldn't be, and I have to try and live with that."

"This isn't your fault, Isak."

"Maybe."

Silence settled around them, and Tuva wanted nothing more but to be held by her husband. She hesitated to reach for him, fearing he would reject her. She knew she couldn't handle it if he did, so she willed him to make the first move. He didn't.

Her shoulders slumped forward, and she turned toward the door. "I guess I will go help with breakfast."

"I'll be there in a minute," Isak said.

Tuva opened the door and paused, hoping he would say or do something to show he still cared for her, still wanted her. When he didn't, she heaved a sigh and shut the door behind her. She tried to push the ache in her heart aside but failed miserably.

Bill and Joshua were all packed and making ready to leave. Marriam had insisted they couldn't go without food for their journey, so put together a light lunch. She straightened the last of the food in the small basket while Tuva held it steady. Then Tuva scooped up the basket and walked with Marriam down to the dock.

She peered at her husband as they neared the men, but he didn't look her way. She tried not to show she was breaking apart inside and thought she was getting away with it until Bill's expression explained otherwise.

Marriam glanced at Tuva, patted her on the hand, and whispered, "Give him time."

Nodding, Tuva stepped forward and handed the basket of food to Joshua. "For your journey, gentlemen."

"Thank you, my dear," Joshua said. He kissed the top of her hand. "Until we meet again."

Tuva nodded and turned to Bill. She held out her hand, and he held it gently between both of his. She was about to release her hand when he said. "Take care of yourself, Tuva."

"And you too," Tuva said.

Bill let her hand drop and walked over to Isak. He held out his hand and Isak hesitantly clasped it.

"Don't hurt her," Bill said. "She deserves nothing but the best."

"You don't have to tell me that," Isak said. "But under the circumstances, I will let your insolence slide."

Bill nodded, smiled, and pulled Isak into a bear hug. "Be safe, my friend."

Isak patted him on the back. "You as well."

The men pulled apart and Bill climbed on board. He and Joshua thanked everyone for their hospitality. Joshua indicated he was looking forward to the family's future endeavors with him, and they were off.

Tuva watched them sail away until they rounded the bend along the shore. She decided she needed some space and went for a walk.

She was just about out of earshot when Wally said, "You know, Isak, you are going to blow this if you can't stop being so pigheaded."

Tuva didn't wait to hear what her husband had to say, and hurried her steps. She walked along the path through the forest, stopping when she happened upon wildlife. She studied different plants and flowers and paused when she caught an occasional glimpse of her lake. The weight of the conflict with her husband lifted some, and she started back toward home.

She was rounding a bend in the trail when she happened upon Isak. He was standing at the edge of the trail, looking out at the water beyond. He didn't seem to hear her, so Tuva tried not to startle him as she grew closer to him. Thinking he either didn't hear her or was ignoring her, she thought about just passing by him and continuing toward home.

Attempting to sneak past, she flinched when he said, "I don't know what I'm supposed to say right now."

"I don't know either," Tuva said.

"On the one hand, I can't get the picture of the two of you holding each other out of my mind. But on the other, I can't help but think about you being battered and bruised and I wasn't there. He was," Isak said, anguish dripping from his voice.

"I wasn't holding him. He was holding me."

"Maybe, but you allowed him to."

"You're right. I did. I shouldn't have done that. But it wasn't from a place of longing or love for him," Tuva said. "The real question I have, though, is this. Will you ever be able to hold me again?"

"What?" Isak asked. "I don't even understand that question."

"You have barely touched me."

"I'm not sure ..." Isak trailed off.

"I see," Tuva said, feeling the crack in her heart deepen. She turned and started walking back down the path.

"Where are you going?"

"I can't stand here and not know what you're thinking, Isak. This has been hard enough."

"What's that supposed to mean?"

"I don't know. I guess we both need to figure some things out."

"Wait, I don't understand what that means," Isak said.

But Tuva didn't stop. She kept walking until she rounded another bend in the trail before running toward home. Once there, she flung herself on her bed and allowed the pain to pour out with her tears. She wasn't sure how long she was there, but knew it had been a while based on the shadows in the room.

Finally, with determination, she got up, washed her face, and straightened her clothes.

"Pull yourself together," Tuva said, and went in search of Marriam.

Chapter Twenty-Five

Dear Nora,

It's hard to believe summer is almost ending again soon. Your new husband sounds wonderful. I wish I was there so I could meet him. Things with Isak and I are not much better. We seem to just dance around each other's pain. And he won't talk to me. The copper mine hasn't been successful, but Isak refuses to give up. I'm thankful for the small income our other endeavors bring in. Since we can stay afloat with everything else going on and with money put aside already, I think he will probably keep trying a little longer with his copper.

In answer to your question about babies. We have not been fortunate in that area. I was beginning to wonder if perhaps something was wrong with me. And now Isak barely sleeps in bed with me.

My heart aches, dear sister. I miss you so.

Don't tell Mamma and Pappa about my troubles, please, but give them my love.

Tuva

Chapter Twenty-Six

The sun slid behind dark clouds just as Tuva picked the last of her harvest for the day. The nights were coming quicker, and she found she was dreading winter. At least with the beautiful weather during the spring, summer, and fall, she could spend most of her time outdoors. But with winter coming, she was worried about the forced time indoors with Isak.

Marriam and the rest of the family had been wonderful, and encouraged her to continue to give Isak time, but she was growing weary of it. It seemed like the longer they didn't resolve the issue, the deeper the wedge was between them. A flash of light lit up the sky in blues and purples, and a deep rumble sounded in the distance.

The wind picked up, and she studied the clouds that were building overhead. A storm was coming, and it was going to be a bad one.

"Tuva," Marriam hollered from the porch. "Can you grab some green beans for dinner?"

"Will do," she said, and plucked the beans from the vines. She had finished settling the vegetable in her basket when the waves built, crashing against the beach and dock. The sky grew darker, and large drops fell on her arms.

Tuva ran toward the house. She just reached the porch when the heavens opened and poured on the little cabin. Tuva could barely see the edge of the shore now, but she could hear the ruckus it was creating.

Marriam flung open the door and shouted, "Gracious, child. Come in. That porch won't keep you from getting wet in this kind of storm."

Following her mother-in-law inside, Tuva said, "I hope our men are almost home. This storm is going to be a bad one."

"I had the same thought. Go dry off and warm up by the fire. I will get supper on," Marriam said, handing Tuva a towel.

Tuva patted at her clothes when the front door flew open with a crash. She jumped and almost dropped the towel when four soaked men walked into the cabin. Tuva locked eyes with Isak, and she smiled, hoping to get some reaction from him. There was almost a lift to his lips before he moved to secure the door. When he turned back around, he wouldn't look in her direction.

Tuva focused on the fire and pushed away any hopes for reconciliation again tonight. Tuva handed the towel to Wally, and he thanked her with a wink. They talked about the day while Tuva snuck glances at Isak. She watched as he brushed at the dampness on his clothes before he helped his mother with the dinner preparations.

Tuva felt bad he was helping instead of her, so she went into the kitchen area and asked how she could help. Isak mumbled something about wanting to go change, and let her take over stirring the mashed potatoes. Her face fell when he walked away without more of a greeting.

"This is just ridiculous," Tuva said. She threw the spoon on the counter and stomped after her husband.

The wind caught the door when she flung it open, and she had a hard time closing it behind her. She was crossing the porch when the lake crashed against the beach and up toward the cabin, reaching further than it ever had before. Tuva paused, watching another wave build momentum to pound against anything in its path. It kissed the ground just below the porch, before receding to build again.

More water rushed toward her, spraying her lightly, before landing just shy of where she was standing. Tuva's stomach sank, and she feared they were going to lose everything, only this time by the harsh waves of her beautiful lake.

"Tuva," Isak hollered at her. "Come on, we have to go inside. This is becoming dangerous, and we need to move our things to higher ground."

"Oh, so now you're speaking to me?" she yelled.

"This isn't the time or place to do this."

"Oh yeah. When is the right time, Isak?"

"I can't do this right now. We need to prepare for what is to come."

"We will do that, but for now, I'm not leaving this spot until you talk to me."

"What do you want me to say?"

"Say anything," Tuva said. "Say you hate me. Say you can't stand to be around me. Just say something."

"Hate you?" Isak hollered. "Why would you think I hate you?"

"Because you don't touch me. You don't talk to me. You won't even look at me half the time."

Isak took a step closer to her. "I could never hate you, Tuva."

"Then what is it?"

"I should have been there for you. But I was so determined to create this perfect life for you, that I let you down."

"You didn't let me down."

Another surge crashed against the side of the porch, knocking Tuva off balance. Isak rushed to keep her upright and their eyes locked. A dam broke between them. Isak jerked her against him and kissed her with an urgency and fierceness she hadn't felt from him before.

A loud crack of thunder ripped open, and a wave battered against them before slamming into the side of the house.

Isak pulled away. "This isn't safe any longer. Run to our room, gather all that you can, and bring it to the main house. I will go tell everyone else to gather items. We will need to make a run for the shed. It is much higher than here, and I think we will be okay there."

All Tuva could do was nod before running into their room. She grabbed two carpet bags from under the bed and filled them both. She tucked items in trunks, hoping they would be okay if they got wet, but would keep them from getting washed away.

Once her chore was complete, she watched her lake overpower the land, and she ran for the kitchen, hoping she would make it in time. The kitchen opened to her, and Wally yanked her into the house, slamming the door, seconds before the water pounded against it.

A look of fear crossed Wally's face and Tuva attempted to reassure him, before jumping into action to help her family plan their escape from the house. Everything was packed, and the family decided it was safer to go out the kitchen door and run around the back. They went two at a time, lugging all the things they were able to gather in such a short time.

Once they were settled in the shed, Marriam set a blanket on the floor. "We might as well eat. It's going to be a long night, and we should get through it on full stomachs."

Josef chuckled and agreed with his wife. He settled next to her and helped prepare plates of food. The family crowded together, eating and talking about nonsense to pass the time.

The storm raged on, and with each swell, Tuva wondered if there would be any home left. Her mind shifted to the moment on the porch, but Isak now sat far away from her. He was huddled in the corner, studying his hands.

Tuva settled next to Marriam and they discussed the garden. They wondered if it was far enough back to be safe. Josef sat with Adam and Wally and talked about the mine, but he looked toward the door with every rumble. Isak sat in silence while he stared at the wall.

"He looks so lost and broken, Marriam," Tuva said. "How did I not see that before."

"Because you have been trying to heal too, honey. And that's okay," Marriam said.

"He kissed me," Tuva blurted out.

"When?" Marriam asked.

"Just before the waves started to crash against the house," she said. "I thought it meant that finally we would be able to talk about things, but now look. He is huddled in the corner, and won't look at me yet again."

"Maybe you need to go to him," Marriam said gently.

"But what if he rejects me?"

"Then you will know."

Tuva shuddered, but the memory of the kiss on the porch spurred her on. She gathered her courage and went to her husband. She knelt in front of him, gathering his hands in hers. He didn't pull away, but he also didn't look at her.

"You okay?" Tuva asked.

"I failed you again, Tuva," Isak said.

"Failed me?" she asked. "What on earth are you talking about? You have never failed me."

"I failed you when I couldn't keep you safe in that horrible storm when we crossed to America. We lost the farm to the fire. Then your attack, and you had to seek comfort in another man's arms. The mine isn't producing as I hoped, so many people are panicking and giving up on life here and I don't know what to do about our mine. Now the home I built for you is getting destroyed with each passing wave."

Tuva wrapped her arms around him and held tight. "You listen to me, Isak Nilsson. There isn't a soul alive that could have prevented any of what has happened to us. To me. I didn't seek comfort the way you have imagined from any other man. He was just a friend. I only ever wanted, and will ever want, you."

Isak's shoulders collapsed. He buried his face into her chest and his anguish poured out.

Tuva held him until his body stopped shaking. When he was more composed, she gently gathered his face in her hands and kissed him softly.

"We are in this together. If you would just let us be together in it," she said.

It was Isak's turn to wrap his arms around her, settling her on his lap.

"You are such an amazing woman, my Tuva."

Tuva's heart skipped a beat at his endearment. She hadn't heard him call her that in so long.

"And you are an amazing man, my Isak."

"I love you," he whispered against her ear.

"And I love you," Tuva said, heat rushing through her body. "So very much."

"Please tell me now and I will forever bury this between us. Was there a time, maybe even a little, that you loved Bill?" Isak asked.

"Never in the way you mean. Not once," she said. "I have always, and will always, love only you."

Isak cradled Tuva long into the night. As the winds died down, leading the way for dawn to arrive, Tuva woke in her husband's arms. She surveyed the little shed and realized everyone else was still asleep. Growing restless, she decided to go check on her home.

The smaller ripples of water indicated her lake was no longer pounding away at the cabin, so she knew it would be safe. Tuva snuck out the shack door, careful to close it gently behind her. The sky was still cloudy, but the rain had stopped. She wandered around to the front of the home, stepping over debris. Her stomach turned over and a weight rested on her heart.

Windows were shattered, boards were broken, and walls were caved in. The front porch was shredded and the porch between her little room and the main cabin was swept away. She climbed into her little room and checked her trunks. They had shifted, but everything inside was safe.

The bed was jostled into a new position, but was intact. She righted the dresser that had fallen against the bed and heaved a sigh, realizing it wasn't damaged beyond repair. She twirled around, listening to the crunch of glass under her feet. It was brighter in the room, from the light pouring through holes in the walls.

Hearing voices, Tuva went out to greet her family and offer encouragement. Marriam clung to her husband, but was rigid against the grief that emanated from her. Tuva knew it was from her losing yet another home.

Adam, Wally, and Isak stumbled about, and for the first time, her family seemed lost. Tuva wasn't sure if she had the strength to handle her family fracturing. She decided it was up to her to take charge.

"Marriam, how about you gather up any food you can find, and start making some breakfast," she said. Everyone blinked at her, but seemed thankful for someone offering a direction.

"Josef and Wally, you gather some firewood and start a fire. Adam and Isak, start making a list of things we can repair and clean, so that we can sleep in our home tonight. And I will start some coffee," Tuva said, pushing up her sleeves.

They followed her instructions, bustling about while she kept an eye on them. It was a start. She was glad she had mustered the courage to give them what they needed. Her gaze was drawn to the water, and she remembered what Minwaadizi had said to her about the lake. It could be ferocious. It could take away. But it would also provide comfort when she needed it the most.

Tuva was pulled to the shoreline where she took off her shoes and stockings. She let the cold liquid swallow her feet and breathed in the damp air. A laugh formed in the back of her throat, and she couldn't stop it from escaping.

She lifted her arms in the air and closed her eyes. "Give us what you've got, my beautiful gichi-gami. This is our home too, and we will not be swayed."

A tiny ripple brushed against the bottom of her skirt, as though in response.

Tuva opened her eyes, wrapping her arms around herself. "You are so beautiful, even when you raise yourself against us."

Chapter Twenty-Seven

The sound of hammers echoed through the bay while Tuva climbed higher on the ridge of the point. She had decided to explore new parts of their land with each walk after the storm. The ground seemed to level out and stay that way for a bit as she walked toward the center.

Crashing against boulders drew Tuva closer to the edge of the point. She realized it would be high enough here. They would be safe the next time a storm rammed against them. Plus, the view took her breath away.

Tuva gathered her shawl closer and started to walk back the way she came. It didn't take long for her to return to where her husband was patching walls. By the time she was standing next to him, she had made up her mind.

"Isak," she said, causing him to stop mid swing.

"Yes," Isak said.

"I have decided where to build our home," Tuva said. "Not the family's. Our home. The home for me and you, and for any children we may eventually have together."

"You have decided," he said, with a twinkle in his eye.

"Yes, if you want to come look with me after lunch and check it out, you can," she said. "But we will build our future there. I just know it."

"What about the rest of the family?"

"We can build them homes close by and further up from here. But we will build our home there," Tuva said, pointing toward the ridge.

Isak stood, covered his eyes and looked in the direction Tuva was pointing. "I'm intrigued. I will say that."

"Okay, so after lunch, let's go look?"

"We will go look after lunch."

"Lunch is ready," Marriam called from the doorway of the cabin, and Isak and Tuva couldn't hold their laughter.

Adam rolled his eyes. "You two." But he winked at Tuva when he walked past her.

Lunch didn't take long, and Isak kept his word. Tuva led the way up the side of the ridge to the leveled area.

She walked in circles and asked, "Can't you just picture it? A small cabin about here. We could clear out some of these trees to have a better view of the water at the edge of the point, and then we could carve out a path wide enough for a wagon to fit leading from the dock all the way up to here."

"You do have this all planned out, don't you?" Isak smirked.

"I told you. I have decided. This is where we will build our future. This whole land. This bay. All of it will be our legacy that we pass to our children and grandchildren."

"Are you sure, Tuva?" Isak asked. "So many people have decided to move away from this area. It's just so hard."

"We didn't come this far to give up now."

"I'm not sure what to do if the mine fails," Isak said, looking off into the distance.

"If it fails, we will try something different. And if that fails, then we will try something else," Tuva said, with fists at her side.

Isak regarded his wife, started to say something, but looked at his hands instead.

"Isak, we will make this work. I know we will," Tuva said as her countenance softened. "Remember what our friends told us. If we love this land and this great water, then she will love us back and will provide. I believe that with all my heart. I believe we will do this. We can do this, if we do it together."

Isak shook his head. "I don't know what I did to deserve you, but I'm so glad you are my Tuva."

"So, is that a yes to our home?"

"Did I really have a choice?" he said, with a snort. "Of course, it's a yes. And I'm with you. Together we will make this work."

Chapter Twenty-Eight

Dear Nora,

I have a new home here. This land and water know how to put up a fight, but we are resilient and steadfast in our resolve to stay here. If you were ever able to see this place, you would understand it. It was home the first time I ever saw it. And it will be my home until they lay me in its dirt.

Isak and I are on the mend too. It makes my heart happy. Even though we have had a rough go of it. I'm ever so grateful that we are here. I wish letters weren't so slow to come and go. I wish I could hear how things are with you and your husband. I wish I could see your smiling face.

Give my love to Pappa and Mamma,

Tuva

Chapter Twenty-Nine

Spring 1861

The dining area of the boarding house was bustling with patrons as Tuva sipped on her coffee and read the newspaper. She and Isak and the brothers were in Duluth for a supply run, but the two-week trip turned into a month-long stay while Isak finalized the new agreement with the General Store. He and Adam were off signing the contract that morning while Wally kept Tuva company at the boarding house.

Tuva couldn't believe what she was reading. She placed the paper on the table and looked over at Wally.

"What do you think of this?"

"I don't know what to think," Wally said, "but I know that something needs to be done to fix this problem."

"I agree," Tuva said, "but war is the worst possible answer for all of this."

"Maybe," he said, "but I can't think of just sitting by and doing nothing to help."

"You're not thinking about signing up?"

"And why not," Wally said. "I have a sense of pride for this place, especially being a part of Minnesota becoming a state. I love this country, and the president has asked for volunteers to fight."

"Promise me you won't make any rash decisions until we have had a chance to discuss this as a family. Please, Wally."

"I will think about it."

"Please," she repeated.

"Fine. I won't decide anything without discussing it with the family."

Adam walked into the café and found his way to the table.

He plopped down, saying, "Well, I signed up. I'm heading to Minneapolis in a few days."

"You can't be serious, Adam," Tuva said. "Wally and I were just talking about this, and he promised not to sign up without discussing it with the family and here you go, undermining that whole conversation with this decision of yours."

"I agree with you, Tuva," Adam said. "Wally is much younger, and we should discuss if he should go, but I'm a man, and I have a responsibility to this country."

"Hey, I'm a man," Wally said.

"Barely," Adam said.

"Still makes it true," Wally said.

"We won't discuss any more of it," Tuva said. "Where's Isak?"

"He is talking with Bill and Joshua about some additional plans he has for our boarding house and a possible clearing of the trail so that it's easier for people to pass through our area," Adam said.

"Always looking to future endeavors," Tuva commented. "But that is what has kept us afloat through the panic and the copper mines closing, so we can't really complain, can we."

"It's your fault, really, Tuva," Adam said with a teasing tone. "He's always trying to make you happy."

"Because that is such a hard thing to do," Tuva said, rolling her eyes.

Wally kicked under the table, hitting Tuva squarely on the shin.

"Ouch. Wally," Tuva screeched.

Adam smacked his brother on the back of his head. "See why we need to discuss things about you, and the decisions you make? You can't even kick me under the table right."

Wally started to respond, but Tuva cut him off, "Boys, seriously now. It's a miracle I don't have more bruises or even broken bones with you pounding at each other all the time, and half the time missing."

Adam and Wally blinked before erupting into laughter, which is how Isak found them. He rolled his eyes at Tuva, and she couldn't hold back her own amusement. Her smile faltered as Bill joined the group. It had been a couple of years since the situation had resolved itself with him, but Tuva always hesitated when she saw him, even now.

"We came to fetch you, and obviously save you from the boys," Isak said. "Besides, we need to get going or we won't make it back home before dark."

Tuva stood, gathered her things, making sure to tuck the newspaper into her bag. She knew Josef would want to read it. Adam went to pay the bill for their breakfast, and Tuva and Wally followed Isak out of the café.

"Bill, it's good to see you," Tuva said.

"Always so gracious, Tuva," he responded.

"How have you been?" Tuva asked.

"I'm joining up," Bill said. "I'm heading out with Adam in a few days."

Tuva's heart skipped a beat, but she forced her countenance to keep from faltering. It was difficult to mask her true feelings, as she thought about three important men in her life going off to war. Things would forever be awkward between her and Bill, but he would always have a special place in her heart.

"That is a sad day for all of us. We will miss you around here."

"Thank you for saying that," he said.

"I mean it, Bill. Sincerely. You know that. At least I hope you do."

Isak cleared his throat and Tuva peered at her husband. As far as they had come, it still made him uncomfortable to discuss things closer to the heart. Especially when Bill's feelings for Tuva leaked into the conversation.

"We should get going," she said.

"It was, as always, a pleasure, Tuva," Bill said. "Adam, I will walk with you to the water to discuss our plans."

"Thank you," Tuva said, linking arms with her husband. They walked arm in arm to their waiting boat and Tuva climbed aboard without any assistance. She settled her things, nestled in her spot, and waited for the men to finish their tasks before casting off.

"One final look, Tuva," Bill hollered from the dock. "Sorry, Isak. Man going to war doesn't always think."

Tuva looked at Isak, and he nodded. Tuva knew she didn't need his permission but asked for it out of respect. She moved to the edge of the boat to get a better view of Bill and waved.

"Please be careful. You need to come home to help us continue to build this little community."

"I will do my best, Tuva," Bill said.

"Hang on, Tuva," Wally said. "We are casting off now."

Tuva prepared for the shift in the boat, but continued to stand. She blew Bill a kiss and lifted her hand in the air.

"Goodbye, my dear friend. Please take care of yourself."

Bill only waved at her, but to Adam said, "I will see you in a few days."

Tuva sat, but could still see Bill watching them sail away. She hoped this wouldn't be the last time she saw him.

Isak settled next to her. "You okay, my Tuva?"

Tuva knew he used his endearment for her to show he wasn't upset over the exchange with Bill, even if it did make him uncomfortable.

Reaching over to squeeze her husband's hand, Tuva said, "You are the best of men, my Isak. Yes, I'm fine."

"Good," Isak said. He pressed her hand, let go, and walked over to help Adam prepare the sail. "Homeward bound," he hollered.

Giggling, Tuva watched her husband finishing his task, and then stared across the tide. She studied the forest as they sailed, hoping to catch a glimpse of her dear friend Minwaadizi. It had been so long since she had last seen her. Tuva had been told that Minwaadizi had been forced to move with her family to a reservation but hoped it was false information and would eventually stumble on her path again.

As Tuva learned more about how the country had been taken from the people of the land, it made her feel guilty for taking up residence where she did. Makwa's blessing for them to be in her bay helped ease some of that shame. It also gave her a sense of responsibility to do the right thing, always.

She took it upon herself to make sure the Nilssons acted in an honorable fashion, opening their home and businesses to one and all. She took great pride in the family's efforts to build an honorable legacy for their future, preserving the memories of the land, hoping to atone for the wrongs of the past.

The wind blew stronger and Isak said, "With that breeze, we should make excellent time getting home, even with our provisions loading us down."

"Yes," she agreed, but continued to stare into the distance.

"Are you sure you're okay?" he asked.

"Yes, I was just thinking of Minwaadizi."

"It has been so long, hasn't it?"

"Yes, I think about her often."

"Maybe we can cheer you up, and discuss my enlisting to help fight," Wally said.

"How would that cheer me up?" she asked.

"Okay, not cheer up, but get your mind off it?" Wally said.

"You already know my answer. I don't imagine Mamma saying anything differently," Tuva said.

"You might be surprised," Adam said. "Mamma is really big on family honor."

"She won't be big on letting half her family go to war," Tuva said. "At least that is how I feel about it. But if you must go, you must go. Even though it will break my heart."

The conversation faded as the men turned to their activities of navigating the vessel. Tuva forced herself to focus on the beauty enveloping her, and the rest of the trip home was uneventful. When they arrived at their home dock, Marriam and Josef were anxiously waiting for them.

"Goodness, I wasn't sure if you were going to make it today after all," Marriam said, lifting a basket from Tuva's arms. The women hugged and walked off the dock, leaving the heavy lifting to the men.

Tuva paused once on dry land and took in her surroundings. It looked so different from the first time she had arrived here. The little cabin shredded in the storm was no longer there.

A larger cabin had been built further up into the forest, well away from the shore. It was where Josef, Marriam, Wally, and Adam resided. Two smaller one room cabins were scattered about, which were used as guest houses for those passing through the area.

A small building off to the left and a little closer toward the water was used as a store. People from miles around came to trade goods, buy bread and jams, and at times, furniture the Nilssons made. Some even took advantage of the vegetables available from the large garden Tuva had created.

Most settlers had left the area in the Panic of 1857, but those who stayed relied on fortitude and the Nilssons' supplies they sold or traded. They were well known by those who continued to live along the shores of the great lake.

Tuva looked up toward the ridge, and a wide grin spread across her face. Every time she caught even a glimpse of her home, it made her giddy with joy. Isak had kept his promise and built them a two-bedroom cabin with a loft and a nice size kitchen and living area. They had kept as many of the trees as possible, so it was hard to see from where she was standing, but she knew it was there, and couldn't wait to sleep in her own bed.

"Are you wondering how you are going to get all your new things up to your cabin?" Marriam asked with a hint of laughter in her voice.

"No, this place just always takes my breath away, especially when I have been away from it," Tuva said. She adjusted the basket she was carrying and followed Marriam up the path toward the main cabin.

Tuva deposited Marriam's requested purchases on the porch, then went to load the small wagon awaiting them. It wasn't a long way, but having something to help carry their items made the trips less cumbersome when bringing supplies home.

The men made a quick chore of unloading, and Isak was heading toward their cabin with their own supplies. Tuva could have ridden with him, but she always enjoyed the walk, and today wasn't any different. Besides, she was trying to come up with a plan on how to tell her husband of the little secret nestled below her heart.

Thinking of the baby, Tuva placed her hand on her stomach and warmth ran through her body. They had been hoping for a baby for so long, and she prayed the next six months would go quickly. Her only concern was the timing, which meant the baby would be born on the cusp of when the weather changed.

A rustling in the brush led to a small rabbit scuttling across the path. Tuva jumped and giggled at being startled by it. This brought her back to the task of unloading and putting away their new supplies, and she quickened her pace. She was excited to go through everything.

"Tuva, you coming?" Isak called from the cabin.

"Almost there," Tuva replied, cresting the small hill giving way to the most spectacular view of her cabin with the lake as a backdrop. "Oh," Tuva said. She was always surprised at how this view affected her, even though she had seen it almost every day for the last four years.

Isak met Tuva, saying he would escort her the rest of the way.

"You always look so beautiful here," Isak said, cradling Tuva's hand against the crook of his arm.

"I don't look beautiful other places?" she asked with a smirk.

"It's just that here you look so at peace and happy," Isak said. "It's almost as if you're glowing."

"I may have another reason for the glow," Tuva said.

Isak stopped and swung Tuva to face him. He looked down at her belly, back into her eyes, and asked, "Do you mean?"

Tuva nodded. "Yes. Finally, we will be parents."

Isak let out a whoop and pulled Tuva into a gentle embrace, before picking her up to swing her around. His face went from happiness to fear, and he set Tuva down abruptly.

"Wait, should I have done that? Did I just hurt you? Did I just hurt the baby?"

Laughter exploded out of her. "I'm not fragile as glass, Isak. Me and the baby are fine."

"Well, in that case." Isak twirled her around one more time.

"It may not hurt us, Isak, but you will make me dizzy if we keep spinning around," she said.

He placed Tuva back on the ground, but didn't let her go. He held on to her the rest of the way to the cabin. When they reached the porch, he kissed her passionately.

"Should I come back?" a voice asked.

When Tuva looked around to see who had spoken, she noticed Adam was hanging back.

"You're fine, brother," she said, before swatting Isak on the behind. "You guys have work to do. I will go air out the cabin."

Isak whistled a happy tune about love and family, and started toward the wagon.

"What got into him?" Adam asked. "Are your kisses that potent, sister?"

"Mind your manners, Adam," Isak said, smacking his brother on the back of his head playfully.

Adam threw his hands in the air, looking confused, and dove into helping Isak. Tuva giggled as she walked into her home. She went around and opened windows and shutters to let in the air and light. She grabbed a towel and dusted off a few surfaces. She made a short inventory of the food items she had, so she knew what she needed to gather from the root cellar before starting dinner.

"Mamma said to let you know that you and Isak are expected for dinner," Adam said, dropping a crate of goods in the kitchen. "She said, no sense in you trying to cook after a long day on the water."

"That sounds wonderful," Tuva said. "One less thing I need to worry about right now."

Adam nodded and went back outside for another load. Tuva decided to go ahead and start unpacking the crates of supplies and pushed up her sleeves. She knew if she got to work right away, she would be done by the time they would be expected for dinner.

The unpacking went smoothly, and Tuva pulled the last crate into the bedroom that would one day be her baby's room. She pulled off the top and picked up the first package. She unfolded it and gently rubbed her fingers on the material. She planned to make little baby clothes with it and couldn't wait to get started.

Wrapping the paper back around the material, she put it on the floor next to her and continued to inventory all the other items, making sure nothing had been overlooked. Everything in the crate was specific to her pregnancy or items to be created for their baby, and she would need every piece.

Moisture formed at the corner of her eye as she thought about her mamma and sister. An ache spread in her heart, knowing they wouldn't be there when her baby came.

A small knock in the doorway signaled Isak's presence. "I'm going to run the wagon back down to the stable unless you want to ride it down for dinner."

"No, I would rather walk," Tuva said.

"I figured you might," he said. Then, changing the subject, he asked, "Are you missing your mamma?"

"You always read me like a book. Yes, and Nora." Tuva wiped at her eyes.

"I know they wish they were here," he said. "Or you were there, I guess."

"I suppose so."

Isak grew quiet before asking, "Do you wish you would have stayed? That we would have stayed. In Sweden I mean."

Tuva looked out the window at the wonder of her land. "Not for a second. I was meant for this place. Our family was meant for this place. I love our home."

Isak went and kissed the top of Tuva's head. "I'll be right back. I love you, my Tuva."

"I love you too, my Isak," Tuva said, and Isak went off to complete his chore.

Tuva pulled herself together and continued going through the crate of goods. Once she was finished, she tucked everything in the built-in cabinet, shut the door, and left the room to freshen up for dinner.

By the time Isak returned, Tuva was sitting on her front porch rocker, staring at the majesty of the view before her. She sensed her husband's presence before she saw him and beamed at him. Her heart flip-flopped as she read the expression on his face. It was love mixed with desire, and she wondered if they would make it to dinner on time.

Isak leaned down to kiss her, and she moaned, wanting more. Isak started to lead Tuva inside when she noticed Wally walking toward them.

"Change of plans," Tuva said. "Your brothers really do have the worst timing today."

Stepping away from her, Isak cleared his throat and asked, "What is it, Wally?"

"I feel like I have interrupted something here," Wally said, with a smirk.

"You could say that," Isak said with a look of annoyance aimed at his brother.

"As much as I would love to leave you to it," Wally said, "I came to talk with you about me joining the war effort. The president asked for volunteers, and I think I should go. It's just that after our conversation this afternoon, Tuva, I'm suddenly nervous about talking with Mamma and Pappa about it.

"Come sit," Tuva said.

When they were all settled, Wally said, "I know you have strong feelings about me going. But I do too. I couldn't live with myself if I didn't do this. Isak needs to stay here and help Mamma and Pappa, and he has you. But our family needs to do our part and with Adam going, that just makes me more determined to go, too."

"That is quite a speech," Tuva said. "How could I say no after that?"

"Will you support me?" Wally asked.

"I understand your feelings, little brother," Isak said. "So, you have my support."

"And as much as I want to say no, you have my support too," Tuva said.

"That makes me feel better," Wally said. "I know with everyone else supporting me, Mamma and Pappa will, too. I hope."

"We will know soon enough," Tuva said.

"It is getting late now," Isak said. "We should make our way down for dinner."

"Let me grab my shawl," Tuva said, and disappeared into the cabin. When she reemerged, Wally and Isak had wandered off a little and looked deep in conversation. Isak eventually placed his hand on his little brother's shoulder and squeezed it. After letting go, he noticed Tuva, and walked back toward her.

"Giving some brotherly advice?" Tuva asked.

"You could say that. It was more of a, don't die on us speech. But how could we not support him and his courage to fight." Isak said.

Tuva linked her arm with her husband's. "We should go and face the elders then."

Wally paled and Isak howled as Wally fell in step with them. The three made their way down to their parents' cabin, where Marriam had prepared a feast of walleye, mashed potatoes, green beans, and corn bread. The aroma greeting them made Tuva's stomach growl, and she giggled.

Marriam looked over at her daughter-in-law with a quizzical expression, but didn't say anything. The family dove into filling plates and getting settled for a delicious meal. The conversation started with the day's journey, turned to the guests who had just left, and went into how they were excited to get going on the garden in a month or two.

Wally took a big bite of food, and mumbled, "I'm answering the president's call and joining the war effort."

Marriam paused with her fork halfway to her mouth, looked over at Tuva, and back to Wally, before asking, "Did you just say what I think you just said?"

"Probably," he said, gathering another bite of food on his fork.

"Were you going to discuss this with us?" Josef asked.

"I'm discussing it now," Wally said, and stuffed his fork into his mouth.

"I'm joining too," Adam said, watching his parents over the glass he hovered just below his mouth.

"When was all this decided?" Marriam asked. "Tuva, Isak, say something."

"What can we say, Mamma," Isak said. "They are grown men, compelled to defend their country. Convicted to answer their president's call to action. Even if it means war."

"I brought our family to this country to live a peaceful life. To prosper. I never intended to watch my sons go off to war," Josef said. He slammed his fork on his plate and pushed away from the table, the chair scrapping loudly on the floor. He stomped over to the window and peered out.

"You are upsetting your father, boys," Marriam said.

"I can't change that," Wally said, "but I believe I'm doing the right thing."

Marriam took a big gulp of her water and said, "Tuva, you haven't said a word. What do you think of this?"

"It pains my heart, but how can I stop them from doing what they believe to be right?" she said.

"I forbid this," Josef yelled.

Adam and Wally started shouting their protests. Marriam tried to calm her boys while Josef matched their defiance with his own. Isak tried to interject here and there but was shut down by his father. Tuva watched, trying to figure out how to help without making it worse.

"I'm pregnant!"

The whole room stilled, and everyone turned toward Tuva.

"What did you just say?" Wally asked.

"You heard me," Tuva said. "I'm pregnant. And as such, I would prefer it if we would handle this in a calm manner."

The whole room erupted again, only this time with joy and congratulations. Handshakes, claps on the back, and hugs were passed around.

When everyone settled, Tuva said, "Look, this is hard. Sending our boys off to war isn't my favorite thing, either."

Pausing, she placed her hand on her stomach. "I think of this precious bundle growing inside of me, and I can't imagine having to face something like this, when he or she goes off to war, or into the world, for that matter. But Wally and Adam have thought this through, and as much as it pains me, I believe we need to support them in this. And then pray for their safe return."

Marriam wiped at her eyes. "When do you leave?"

"A couple of days," Adam said.

Josef studied his younger sons, and just when Tuva thought he was going to try to sway them not to go, he said, "I guess we need to make the most of the time we have." He abruptly pushed away from the table a second time, but left the cabin, slamming the door behind him.

"Give him time to get used to this," Marriam said.

"We don't have a lot of time," Wally said.

"Yes, I know, son," Marriam said, "but your father worked hard to bring us here for a better life. Joining a war was not part of that plan. It's hard for him to watch his children go off to fight because he loves each one of you so much."

"We know, Mamma," Adam said.

"Yes, we know he loves us, and we love him, too," Wally said.

"But you still have to go, and we know that now too," Marriam said.

"It's a hard reality to face," Tuva said, reaching across the table to place her hand over Marriam's.

"Thank you for supporting us," Adam said.

"Did we have a choice?" Marriam asked.

Adam looked down at his plate sheepishly, but Wally said, "Yes, you did have a choice. And that is why we thank you."

Chapter Thirty

Dear Sister,

I'm keeping my promise to write. Adam and I are settled and are making ready to fight. A lot of other men here are just like us, volunteers, ready to serve. Rumor has it the war won't last long, so that gives me hope. The food isn't so bad, and neither are our quarters. So, tell Mamma not to worry. Give her and Pappa my love.

Hope you and Isak are good. Keep me updated on my nephew or niece and, of course, other happenings at home. Am being called away for some training. Will write again soon.

Your ever faithful brother,

Wally

Chapter Thirty-One

The wind whipped across the lake, billowing the shirt around Tuva's head, making it difficult to pin down. Once the garment was secure, she bent over to grab the next article of clothing and realized the basket was empty. She was so lost in thought she hadn't realized her chore was now over.

Tuva picked up the basket and started the trek up to her little cabin, but Marriam called out, stopping her progression.

"Tuva, won't you come in for some coffee and visit for a bit?" Marriam asked.

Changing directions, Tuva walked toward Marriam, saying, "That would be lovely. It has been a while since we just sat and visited."

"I thought the same and was ready to take a break in between chores, so I thought, no opportunity like the present."

Tuva chuckled and set her clothes basket on the front porch, before following Marriam inside. Marriam poured a cup for each of them and offered Tuva a biscuit.

"Oh my, it's a regular fika," Tuva said with a giggle. "Did you make seven different types?"

Marriam laughed. "If only I had the time and enough product to do that."

"Should we go sit outside?" Tuva asked. "It's such a lovely day, even if it's a little breezy."

"That's a great idea. I will follow you."

Once Tuva was settled in a rocking chair on the porch, she stared out at the sparkles on the water. The corners of her mouth lifted at the sight. She breathed in the scent of fresh coffee and wildflowers before taking a sip.

"I could sit here the rest of the day," Marriam said, taking a bite of her biscuit.

"I agree," Tuva said. "You know, Marriam, maybe we should sell some of our pastries and biscuits in the store. Not everyone has the capability to bake like you and I are able to. It might be a little something extra people could place an order for or just come and purchase if we have a small selection available."

"What a lovely idea," Marriam said. "Trading could also work. Fish for pastries and biscuits."

"Are you ladies hatching up more schemes to grow our business?" Isak asked, hopping on the porch.

"You heard us?" Tuva asked.

"I did, but we may want to wait until we have more cliental. Boarders are few and far between and we only have the few families we trade with these days," Isak said.

"A thought for the future, I suppose. Especially when we start our town," Tuva said.

"Town?" Isak asked. "What are you talking about?"

"Yes, can't you see it?" Tuva asked. "We could help people finance building here. We could help them get a new beginning. We have more immigrants coming to America from Sweden and other countries looking for a fresh start," Tuva said.

"Hmm," Isak mumbled. "It's a nice thought. But we are getting ahead of ourselves, don't you think?"

"Maybe, just a thought I keep coming back to," Tuva said.

Isak nodded and kissed the top of his wife's head. "Your brain never stops. You are always thinking up something new."

"Maybe."

Tuva giggled when Isak kissed the top of her head again before heading off in the direction of his woodworking shop.

"He doesn't realize how fortunate he is sometimes, I think," Marriam said.

"What do you mean?" Tuva asked.

"All of these ideas. Everything we have started to create here is because of you and your suggestions. I think sometimes he forgets that."

"Perhaps," Tuva said, "but you know how men are these days. A woman couldn't possibly have come up with an idea herself."

Marriam snorted. "And yet, where would our men be without us?"

"Exactly," Tuva agreed. "Although, in all fairness, Isak does listen to me for the most part."

"You are correct," Marriam said with a twinkle in her eye. "He must have had a good upbringing."

Tuva chuckled, sipped the last of her coffee, and set it down on the little table next to her. She rocked back and forth, enjoying the comfortable quiet settling in between them. Tuva longed for the day, though, when there would be more people about and more conversations could be had.

Marriam cleared her throat. "I suppose I must get back to work. I have a little more washing to do myself, and then it's almost time to start dinner."

"How about you skip dinner preparations and you and Josef come up and eat with us this evening? It's been a while since you have been by and besides, I have a couple of baby things I made that I would love to show you."

"That sounds lovely," Marriam said. "We will head that way around dinnertime."

"Here, I can help you bring the coffee and biscuit dishes inside," Tuva said.

"Nonsense," Marriam said. "You get along with your chores now. I can manage."

"Okay. See you later this evening," Tuva said with a smile. She gathered her basket, went to check the clothes she had hung to see how close they were to drying, and made the small trek up to her cabin.

The rest of the afternoon went by quickly and Tuva enjoyed making the preparations for dinner for her little family.

Isak walked into the cabin with the clothes basket in hand. "Here you go."

"Thank you," Tuva said, not lifting her head from the pot she stood over. "If you could just go set that on our bed and I will put the clothes away after dinner."

"I can do better than that. I think I can handle putting clothes away," Isak said, walking into their bedroom.

Tuva marveled that she would end up with such a man. A man who helped her with tasks around the house considered women's work. It was so different from her own childhood. Tuva frowned and her shoulders slumped at the thought of her parents and sister. It had been a while since they had come to mind, and it had been even longer since she received a letter from them. She wondered how they were.

She glanced at the mantel over the fireplace where the sketch her sister had created nestled in between two candlesticks. The day she had left Sweden seemed so long ago, and she knew she had grown and changed since moving here. Yet she still longed for the love and affection from her father she never received as a child. And craved a conversation with her mother and sister.

She didn't realize how much missing them had affected her until she became pregnant and marveled at her own love for the child inside her, and how overwhelming it was. She had a hard time reconciling how her father could be so cold and distant all those years. And she struggled with never hearing from her mother.

There was a gentle knock at the front door before it opened to reveal Josef and Marriam entering the cabin. Tuva smiled at her in-laws, who were more parents to her than in-laws, and she was so thankful for them. Realizing their closeness suddenly highlighted the differences in her relationship with her own parents, and the corners of her mouth dipped.

Josef held flowers in his hand, and Marriam had brought a cake. *Of course, they would not have come empty-handed.* Tuva decided she wouldn't allow her sad memories to spoil the evening.

Marriam helped Tuva put the flowers in water while Josef got comfortable by the fireplace. Isak emerged from finishing his chore and went to visit with his father. Tuva could hear the muffled sounds of general conversation from the men as she finished the final details of dinner.

Once done, Tuva placed the dishes on the table and called the men to eat. After everyone was settled, the conversation turned to the war. They hadn't received many letters from Adam or Wally but were trying to keep up with how things were going by reading the newspaper. It was usually a few days old by the time they got it, so the information was out of date.

"Sounds like our boys are on the way to Washington or I guess they are probably there by now," Josef said.

"I saw that," Isak said. "I also heard in town that this group of women made them a feast, celebrated them, and sent them off real nice."

"Yes, Wally mentioned that they all tried to be in matching clothes," Tuva said.

"I heard that too," Isak said. "Um, checkered flannel and black pants and matching hats or something."

"I just hope this ends soon, like everyone keeps saying it will," Marriam said.

"I hope so too," Tuva said.

A loud bang caused Tuva to slosh water over her glass. "Who could that be at such a late hour?"

Isak opened the front door and asked, "May we help you?"

"Yes. I suppose I should introduce myself first. The name is Spencer Olsen, and I worked sometimes for Mr. Culver, Joshua Culver. He wrote me from Washington and instructed me to give you this." Spencer handed Isak an envelope.

"Won't you please come sit, and I will get you a plate," Tuva said, her eyebrows creased together. She went to fetch a plate and piled it high before Spencer had the chance to respond.

"That is mighty nice of you, Mrs.," Spencer said.

Josef grabbed another chair, and when they were all settled, Isak explained the letter to everyone else.

"There was a battle. It was near a place called Manassas," Isak said. "It was the first battle our men saw. And there were casualties."

"Casualties?" Marriam asked. "Any names?"

Isak looked around the table before saying, "There are no names yet." He shifted in his seat. "They are saying it was a great victory for the south and this is just the beginning of more battles to come."

"So, the idea of a quick war is just that, an idea," Josef said.

"It seems so," Isak said.

"Joshua mentioned you have kin folk at the front and said it was imperative that you receive this information right away," Spencer said. "I didn't hesitate to bring it to you. I have been meaning to ride up here, anyway. I'm trying to find a place for me and my family to settle and thought this might be a good opportunity. Do a good deed and scout the area."

"That is so kind of you," Tuva said. "What do you think of our rugged land and water?"

"It's beautiful, that's for sure," Spencer said. "Just not sure about carving out a space like you folks have."

"Are you looking for a place that is already established?" Tuva asked, sending a pointed look in Isak's direction.

"That would be better for my wife, Marcy," Spencer said. "She comes from the city and the rugged land is having to grow on her some. So, something more established would be better."

"Why not just stay in Duluth or go back toward the cities?" Marriam asked.

"We need a fresh start," Spencer said.

"I can understand that," Josef said.

"Perhaps you and I should talk some more about that," Isak said.

"Do you have something in mind?" Spencer asked.

"I do. How about we look around at things in the morning and discuss this topic more," Isak said.

Tuva studied Marriam while the conversation continued, and she wondered if her mother-in-law would be able to keep it together much longer. The news of casualties and not knowing about Wally or Adam was unnerving for all of them, but to share emotions in front of strangers would not be something Marriam would do.

"Perhaps you can help me clear some of these dishes, Marriam," Tuva said, attempting to distract her.

"I would be happy to help," Marriam said, and started to gather plates while Tuva focused on the rest of the dishes.

The men continued to talk, but drifted onto the front porch. Once the front door was closed, Tuva wrapped her arm around Marriam and said, "If you want to cry, go ahead. I know I would like to."

Marriam set the wet rag down in the water and turned into Tuva's arms. "My boys. Oh, my boys."

"I know, Marriam," Tuva said. "Let's not give up on hope, though."

"You're right, of course," Marriam said. "I'm just terrified that this is growing into something bigger, and it will be much longer before we see our boys again. That is if they even come home." Marriam began to weep and buried her face into Tuva's shoulder.

Tuva held tight and let her own tears fall. She couldn't stop her mind from racing to a life without either one of the boys in it. Before she could stop it, Bill flitted across her mind too. She didn't feel the same concern for him as her brothers, but she still wondered if he was safe.

Marriam quieted, pulled away, and without saying a word, dove back into washing dishes. Tuva knew she didn't want to discuss the subject any further, so she concentrated on drying and putting away, until the kitchen was tidy once again.

"I haven't shown you what I made yet," Tuva said, breaking the silence.

Marriam brightened. "Oh yes. Baby things. I would love to see what you have created."

"Why don't you go sit by the fireplace, and I will bring out the items to you."

"Nonsense. I may have had a moment, but I'm fine now," Marriam said. "Lead the way."

"Right this way then."

Tuva showed Marriam the small articles of clothing and the blanket she had made. She also shared her other plans for further baby clothes, blankets, and Marriam grew misty eyed again.

"I'm so sorry if I'm upsetting you further," Tuva said.

"No dear," Marriam said. "I'm so delighted by all that you are showing me. I can't wait to meet the precious bundle you are carrying. Sharing this with me has lightened my load for a little bit."

Tuva hugged her mother-in-law and yawned loudly. They both chuckled and decided it was time to collect the men and say their goodnights. As Tuva walked her mother-in-law out, she was glad she was able to relieve some of Marriam's pain by sharing the baby items with her.

Waving at the departing man on horseback, Tuva prayed silently for things to come. Isak had taken her idea of having other people settle here and had given Spencer a proposal for a future in their little cove. They could rent the house already built for Marriam and Josef, and help in the store, plus other various jobs. They would build another cabin for Marriam, Josef, and the boys, a small distance from their own up on the ridge.

With Adam and Wally gone, it was becoming more difficult for Isak to stay on top of things. Especially since it was past time for Josef to slow down. Tuva had suggested Spencer take on even more, but Isak had said she shouldn't get ahead of herself.

Spencer was going to take their offer back to Marcy, and see what she thought about it before deciding, but he seemed excited about the prospect as he rode away. Tuva mumbled something about having things to do and started to walk back toward their cabin.

"Hold on just a minute, my Tuva," Isak said.

"Yes," Tuva said, turning around to face him.

"This is probably one of your best ideas yet," he said.

"Oh," Tuva responded, "I would like to think all my ideas are good."

"They are all good ideas, but I do like this one especially." Isak paused. "I really am loving the idea of starting our own community. What a legacy to pass on to our children. To that child nestled inside you. And for our grandchildren."

Tuva snaked her arms around her husband's waist, hugging tight. "It truly is a wondrous idea. Even if it was mine."

Isak whooped as he pulled Tuva into a heated kiss.

Chapter Thirty-Two

Dear Sister,

We are alive. Adam and I are both okay, and I know you will worry for Bill, so I'm happy to say he is also alive. I can't write more right now, but wanted to at least let you know that.

Give my love to everyone in the family.

Your ever faithful brother,

Wally

Chapter Thirty-Three

The sun was shining brightly as Tuva finished weeding the last row in her garden. She had wanted to finish it the day before, but the fatigue from her pregnancy won out. Tuva was disappointed because she was hoping to assist Marriam in making the cabin ready for their new neighbors, but she just couldn't do it.

Spencer and Marcy were moving in today, and Tuva was excited about the prospect of having neighbors again besides family. Marriam and Josef were going to live in the spare bedroom while their new cabin was being built. The plan was to have the new cabin completed by the time the baby comes but in the meantime, having an extra pair of hands for housework would be nice, especially as time went on.

Tuva was happy she was able to make quick work of the last of the weeding. She gathered her tools and started to walk toward the garden shed. She glanced at the cabin as Marriam walked off the porch.

"Let me help you put those away and then we'll go pick some flowers for our new neighbors before lunch," Marriam said.

"I love that idea," Tuva said. "Sorry I wasn't able to help you with the last of the cabin preparations."

"Goodness no. I may be old, but I do remember what it was like when I was pregnant," Marriam said.

"Was it awful for you?" Tuva asked.

"There were times I had to stay in bed all day," Marriam said. "So, I admire your strength in pushing through your hard days."

Tuva flushed at the praise her mother-in-law was bestowing on her. "I guess I feel like I don't have a choice."

"Perhaps, but now that Josef and I will be living with you for a bit, I hope you'll allow me to help you so you can rest if you need it," Marriam said, stuffing the tools in their designated spots. "Now come along, and let's go pick some flowers."

Tuva enjoyed the stroll and flower picking before they made their way back to the cabin for lunch. The men were already there munching on their meal.

"You must have been hungry," Tuva said.

Marriam laughed. "A man's stomach will sometimes force him to do things he wouldn't normally do."

Tuva joined Marriam in her glee before taking a plate and dishing her own food. They finished eating and were wrapping up the lunch dishes when Isak indicated he thought he heard a call from the bay.

"Surely they're not here yet," Josef said. "That would mean they left right at dawn."

Tuva walked out to the porch. "Well, they must have left at dawn, for they are here."

The family walked down the ridge, arriving at the dock as the boat came to rest there. Spencer secured his vessel before helping his wife down. He stood proudly next to the tiny woman and introductions were made all around.

Tuva felt sorry for Marcy because as much as she tried to put on a brave face, she looked terrified.

"It's so wonderful to have you here, Marcy," Tuva said. "I so look forward to getting to know you.

"That is so kind of you to say," Marcy said.

"Come, let's get you up to your new home and make sure it will work for you before you get settled," Tuva said. "We will leave the men to unload."

Marcy gathered a small bag and a basket and started to walk next to Tuva. Marriam flanked Tuva and offered her welcome too. When they got to the front porch of the cabin, Marcy stopped and stared.

"Is everything okay?" Tuva asked.

"Yes. I just. Oh goodness. Please forgive me," Marcy said. "I was not expecting to see such a beautiful cabin. Our last residence was not this lovely."

"We are so pleased you like it," Tuva said.

"Let's hope you still feel this way when you go inside," Marriam said with a teasing tone.

Marcy giggled, and Tuva could tell some of the woman's nerves had eased. Tuva followed Marcy and Marriam into the cabin and stood back, allowing Marriam to show their new neighbor around. Marcy walked around with a look of wonderment, and beamed at the flowers sitting on the table while she ran her fingers on the soft petals.

"These are so lovely, thank you, ladies," Marcy said. "I wasn't sure what to expect. Spencer, of course, praised this plan, and he was so excited about it. But he was excited about moving to Duluth too and that didn't turn out as nice as this is starting out to be. Our quarters there were not quite what we were hoping they would be."

"Did you secure something ahead of time?" Tuva asked.

"We thought we had, but that fell through upon our arrival, as did the job he was promised, so we were scrambling," Marcy said. "Thankfully, he found employment quickly and we made do. When we learned of you folks and what you have done here through

Spencer's employer, he became excited and decided to make plans to create something like what you have created. I told him I couldn't handle another scheme, but he decided to talk me into this at least."

"Well, we are glad you are here," Marriam said.

"I think if I hadn't heard so much about you folks, I wouldn't have come," Marcy said.

"Hopefully, you are finding what you have heard to be true," Tuva said.

"That and then some," Marcy said. "You folks have a reputation in town. A really good one. Hard workers. Kind people. You have a sort of status or something."

"That seems silly to me," Tuva said. "We are just people."

"True, but you know how people talk," Marcy said, "and since you are great friends with Joshua Culver, um, it is to be expected that you are the people to know or want to meet."

Isak walked into the cabin with a trunk and asked, "Where would you like for me to put this?"

"Please forgive me, ladies," Marcy said. "I must focus on getting my house in order."

"Of course," Tuva said. "Oh, and you are invited up to our home for dinner. No sense in trying to figure out a meal after a long day like today."

"You are too kind," Marcy said.

Tuva provided instructions on dinner and left with the promise from Marcy that if she needed assistance with anything, she was to reach out. Tuva made her way up to her cabin to start preparing for an evening of guests and was overcome with joy at having neighbors.

Marriam walked alongside her, but didn't say anything. Tuva assumed she was caught up in her own excitement, but she quickly learned this was not the case.

"I know you're ecstatic at having neighbors," Marriam said as they neared their cabin. "But I'm struggling to share in the same sentiment as you."

"I don't understand," Tuva said.

"It's just we have had all this time with life running smoothly with just us. Very little changes besides our boys going off to war."

"And things are changing, with more changes to come."

"Yes, something like that," Marriam said. "Our family solitude is no more. And as much as I am all for you and Isak, and all your wonderful dreams and plans for this place, I can't help but wish for things to have stayed the same forever."

"I'm so sorry," Tuva said. "I never thought you would be upset by what we are wanting to build here. I guess we should have talked more with you about it."

"No," Marriam said, "you are doing what you believe to be the best for your future. For the family's future. Just try not to grow things too fast."

"Good advice to heed, Mamma."

Marriam beamed. "I love it when you call me that."

"I will have to do it more often," Tuva said. "And please don't think we are trying to leave you and Pappa behind. We want to do this for all of us. Including you two."

"Let's be honest," Marriam said. "Our time here is much shorter than yours. But until it is our time to go, we will support you. Even if I must grieve over what was."

"I so treasure you."

"And I you, my daughter."

Changing the subject, Tuva asked, "What did Adam's last letter have to say?"

Marriam's eyebrows creased. "He didn't say much. Just they were on the move, but would write when he could. He seemed okay, considering all they are going through."

"Yes, Wally's letters are shorter right now. He seems okay too, but I worry about him," Tuva said.

"This will change him."

"Yes, and I fear it will change him in ways we don't want him to change."

"I have the same fear."

Tuva's eyebrows furrowed as she sat on her porch rocker. She rocked gently back and forth while Marriam sat next to her. Neither spoke and Tuva was content in the silence, for she feared the words that were unspoken between them.

What if he doesn't return at all? What if neither of them returns?

Tuva allowed herself to tip toe around those thoughts for a few minutes before letting out a long breath. "I suppose we should get to work."

"Sounds good to me," Marriam said. "Sometimes hard work is the perfect medicine for forcing fearful thoughts aside."

"I couldn't agree more."

Tuva dove into tidying the cabin before turning to the dinner preparations. Marriam insisted on helping with the finishing touches on the dessert. Tuva accepted her help since she was growing weary. Plus, after the whirlwind of the day, Tuva felt like she needed to freshen up before her guests arrived.

When Tuva took off her dress and laid it on the bed, she was glad she had decided to change. She hadn't realized how much she had spilled down the front of her as she prepared the meal. When Isak came into the bedroom a few seconds later, Tuva was laughing at herself, and he looked at her quizzically.

"I have become quite sloppy in my pregnant state," Tuva said.

"Perhaps, but you are still beautiful," Isak said.

"Even with my rounded belly?"

Isak shortened the distance between them and pulled her into his arms.

"I must say, walking in to see my wife half naked makes me want to send the food down to our new neighbors along with Mamma and Pappa, so I can have you all to myself."

"Isak, hush," Tuva said with a giggle. "Someone will hear you."

"Let them," he said with a provocative look before kissing her.

"You must stop. Besides, it must be so difficult for you to make love to me now, anyway."

"Not difficult at all."

Isak continued his advances, but Tuva pushed him away.

"It is taking all of my willpower not to finish this dance, my Isak," she said as heat coursed through her, "but we have guests arriving at any moment, and I'm not even dressed yet."

"Fine, I suppose duty calls," Isak said. "Perhaps we should rethink this plan of ours of growing our community."

Tuva guffawed. "There will be plenty of time for our dancing later. Even with this plan of ours."

There was a knock at the bedroom door, and Tuva jumped.

"Yes," Isak hollered.

"As much as I love to hear that my children love one another, I see our guests walking this way," Marriam said through the door. "Perhaps you should pause your interlude and join us in the living area to await our guests."

Tuva walked to her wardrobe. "See I told you."

Isak followed and kissed her again until her knees were jelly. She leaned into him and lost her footing. Isak helped steady her, and asked, "Are you sure we couldn't sneak out the back? I'm sure we could find a place in the barn."

"That is a tempting offer," Tuva said, "especially after a kiss like that."

"Children," Marriam hollered. "You do know I can hear you."

Tuva giggled as she grabbed a clean dress and rushed to put it on. Isak tried to help, chuckling along with her. They were still laughing when they walked into the living room, just as their guests knocked on the front door.

Marriam gave Isak a pointed look, but winked at Tuva before answering the front door.

Chapter Thirty-Four

Tuva stared at the letters from Wally. He had written several times, but she received all of them at once. The battles continued to rage. He explained his experiences had opened his eyes as to why she had objected to him going off to war. But in the end, he was still happy he was there, taking a stand for his country.

The harshness of the war Wally described seemed unrealistic compared to the beauty of her surroundings. The trees were full of reds and yellows against the backdrop of the blue water. It made Tuva wish she could paint so she could capture it forever on her wall. Tuva tried to write about what she saw, but her words felt inadequate somehow, because when he received it, he could be in the throes of another battle.

Giving up on her letter writing, Tuva decided to go visit her neighbor and see how they were getting along, having been here for several months now. She knew it had been a difficult adjustment for Marcy in the beginning, but Tuva hoped she had settled and was more comfortable. Tuva wanted this to work as it would give her hope of things to come for their little bay.

Tuva wrapped her shawl around her shoulders and started the trek down the ridge. She didn't get far when she ran into Marcy on the path.

"Oh, Tuva," Marcy said, a little out of breath. "I was just on my way to see you."

"And I was on my way to see you," Tuva said with a laugh.

Falling in step with Marcy, Tuva changed directions and started walking back toward home.

"It's such a beautiful day," she said.

"I agree," Marcy said. "The beauty one finds here is what I love about this place."

"My sentiments exactly."

Lifting the small basket in her hand, Marcy said, "I made some treats, and I thought it might be nice to visit and taste a few of them."

"That sounds like a wonderful idea," Tuva said. "I will put some coffee on."

"That sounds even better," Marcy said.

They walked back to Tuva's, where she set about making coffee, while Marcy got comfortable at the kitchen table. Once the coffee was prepared, Tuva brought the kettle and two small mugs over to the table and sat across from Marcy.

Pouring the coffee, Tuva said, "I must say I'm so excited you came to visit me this afternoon. This is one of the things I have been dreaming of since entertaining the possibility of others settling on our land. I love the idea of a small community coming together."

"That is a lovely thought," Marcy said.

"Have you had a chance to visit Marriam since they moved into their new cabin?" Tuva asked.

"Yes," Marcy said. "Isak does such beautiful work."

"Don't forget, Spencer helped too."

"Only at the supervision of your husband."

"I disagree. Isak had good things to say about Spencer's work, and what I saw was wonderful."

"That is so kind of you to say," Marcy said, taking a sip of her coffee.

"Are you feeling better about the move?" Tuva asked.

"Most days, I feel better about it," Marcy said. "Although the thought of starting a family here makes me a little nervous."

"Yes, I can understand that, but as you see"—Tuva patted her large belly—"we are moving forward with that idea," Tuva said.

"You are due soon, right?" Marcy asked. "Are you not scared?"

"I am, but aren't most women scared when they find themselves pregnant? It is the fear of the unknown I think that heightens those feelings," Tuva said, "and that can lead us to making decisions we regret, or it can lead us to not focusing on the right things."

"Which is what?" Marcy asked.

"The fact that I'm grateful to be living in such a place and am able to have this precious bundle even here," Tuva said.

"That is a wonderful perspective for sure," Marcy said. "I wish I was as strong as you."

Tuva paused, her mug just shy of her lips. "You are as strong as me. We are all as strong as we need to be to help us get through the difficult times. The alternative is that some of the difficult times could have destroyed me, but I refused to let them."

"This way in which you look at things is something I will have to think on more," Marcy said. "I do want this place to work for us."

"I'm so glad you want this," Tuva said. "Wanting this to work is half the battle. Because if you wanted it to fail, it most certainly will."

The conversation turned to the war, and they discussed how Wally and Adam seemed to be doing based on their letters. The headlines were often scary to read in the newspaper and Tuva shared she had decided to not focus on those and instead focus on each letter, as they described a more accurate depiction of how they were doing.

Marcy stayed until their mugs were dry, and shortbreads were gone. She thanked Tuva for such a lovely afternoon and started to head out, when Tuva suddenly hunched over with a gasp. She wrapped her arm around her belly.

"Are you okay?" Marcy asked, rushing to her side.

"I think I'm okay," Tuva said. A sharper pain soared through her abdomen. She leaned against the table. "This can't be. It's too early."

Placing her hand on Tuva's back, Marcy said, "Perhaps it's false labor. My mamma told me that it sometimes happens."

"I don't know," Tuva said, "but something doesn't feel right."

"I will run and get Marriam," Marcy said.

"Yes, please do," Tuva said, sitting in the closest chair.

Tuva rode the next wave of pain and tried to catch her breath, just as Marcy returned with Marriam on her heals. She reached out her hand and clung to Marriam.

"I'm scared, Mamma," Tuva muttered.

"We need to get you to bed, but first let me get it ready for childbirth," Marriam said, after assessing the situation. "Marcy, get some water boiling."

Marcy jumped into action while Marriam ran into the next room. Tuva breathed through the next contraction and silently begged for Marriam to hurry. It didn't take long for her mother-in-law to return, and she helped Tuva start the short trek to her bedroom.

Another stab coursed through Tuva, and she leaned against Marriam, trying not to collapse on the floor. Marriam tightened her grip until Tuva relaxed and started walking forward again. As she stepped foot into her bedroom, liquid gushed from between Tuva's legs, her eyes widened, and she looked over at Marriam.

"I think my waters just broke," Tuva said.

"Well then, we best get you in bed," Marriam said.

"Can I help?" Marcy asked from behind. "The water is going, and I can help you get Tuva settled."

Marriam gave instructions, and after some huffing and puffing on Tuva's part, she was finally nestled on top of the sheets. Tuva started to lean forward to lift her skirts when another jab pierced through her and she fell back against her pillow.

"Just breathe through it, Tuva," Marriam said, calmly caressing Tuva's hand.

Tuva's body eased, and she bent forward to lift her skirts. Her head shot up and she exchanged a panicked look with Marriam.

"That doesn't look right," Tuva said.

"I will agree there is a lot of blood," Marriam said. "Marcy, run and get Isak, and hurry."

Tuva watched Marcy dash out of the room and turned to Marriam. "Am I losing the baby?"

"I don't know yet," Marriam said, "but let's not think about that just now."

Tuva's body tensed again, and she reached for Marriam's hand for support through the next onslaught. Tuva followed Marriam's instructions. As things lessened, she cried out for her mother, and she started to relax again.

"I need to go and check on the water," Marriam said.

"No, please don't leave me."

"I won't be gone long. And I will just be in the next room."

"Please hurry."

"I will," Marriam said, rushing into the next room.

Tuva looked around the room and wished she had changed into her nightgown. It was draped on the cabinet at the foot of the bed. When someone entered the room, she turned to holler at Marriam and ask her for help, but it wasn't Marriam returning. It was Isak. The look of fear on his face broke her heart.

"Goodness, do I look as bad as all that?" Tuva asked.

"Never, my Tuva," he said.

"I'm okay."

"Are you?"

"I will be," Tuva said.

Marriam walked into the room behind Isak, carrying strips of cloth in her hand with Marcy right on her heels.

"What can I do?" Marcy asked, crossing to the other side of the bed.

"I really want to get out of these clothes," Tuva said, as she prepared for another contraction.

"Perhaps in a few minutes, Tuva," Marriam instructed.

When Tuva caught her breath, Marriam and Marcy helped her change, and she tried not to be alarmed at how weak she was. Once she was settled again, she asked for a glass of water, and Marcy left the room. Tuva reached for Isak, and he kneeled next to her, caressing her hand.

"You need to focus on reserving your strength for when things near the end," Marriam said.

"I will do my best," Tuva said.

As the day turned into night, Tuva tried to focus on following directions but grew weaker with each contraction. It was becoming more difficult to concentrate on Marriam's words as another wave of pain flowed through her. The room spun, and she fought blacking out. She clung to Isak's voice until she came out of it once more.

Marriam huddled with Isak and Marcy and whispered intently while Tuva tried to sit up and listen to what was being said. Dizziness took over and she collapsed against her pillow.

"What are you whispering about?" Tuva asked.

"Mamma is just giving us orders," Isak said.

"Don't lie to me, Isak," Tuva said. "Remember, lying to me is not protecting me."

"We are concerned at how much blood you have lost. And we are worried about the baby," Marcy explained.

Isak glared at Marcy.

"I would want to know, and I'm sure she wants to know too," Marcy said.

"Am I going to lose the baby?" Tuva asked.

"I don't know," Marriam said.

Another punch permeated her, and Tuva screamed. Isak ran to her side and coaxed her through the next round. Marriam prepared a cool washcloth and leaned over her when a pounding sounded through the house.

"Oh," Marriam said, dropping the rag on Tuva's chest.

"Who could that be?" Marcy asked.

"Isak, go see who that is. Now," Marriam directed.

Tuva leaned into the coolness of the cloth Marriam rubbed gently over her face, but pulled back when Isak's surprised greeting drifted into her room. Attempting to sit up to get a better view of who it could be, she fell back against her pillow. She tried to focus on anything to stop the room from spinning. As she struggled to bring her surroundings into focus, a faint figure floated toward her, and Tuva wondered if she was dreaming.

"Minwaadizi?" Tuva whispered. "Am I hallucinating?"

Catching movement on the other side of the room, Tuva realized Marcy had backed against the wall with a look of terror on her face.

"You don't need to be frightened, Marcy," Marriam said. "She is our friend."

Minwaadizi sat next to Tuva on the bed and placed a small bag at her side. She ran her fingers along Tuva's abdomen and assessed the liquid pooling in between Tuva's legs.

"I dream of this," Minwaadizi said. "I dream you are dying."

"Am I going to die?" Tuva asked.

"No, my friend," Minwaadizi said. "I'm here."

The pangs began to build again, and she thought she heard a scream just as everything went black.

Chapter Thirty-Five

Hearing voices whispering next to her, Tuva forced her eyes open. She glanced around the room and caught Marriam and Minwaadizi huddled together in the corner. Isak sat next to her on the bed, but he seemed to be focused on what his mother was saying. Tuva lifted her hand to feel her stomach and realized it was no longer taut or solid.

"My baby?" Tuva asked.

Isak looked down on Tuva with so much love and heartache she knew the answer before he could give it.

"No," she cried out. "No."

Isak gathered her into his arms. "I'm so sorry, my Tuva."

Tuva clung to Isak as they wept together until her eyes grew heavy. She settled back against her pillow, wishing for sleep to return. She prayed she would never wake as an unbearable ache coursed through her. It broke her into a thousand pieces, and she wondered if she would ever feel whole again.

"I understand this pain, my friend," Minwaadizi whispered into Tuva's ear. "Rest for now and when you are ready to join us, we are here."

Moisture built in the corner of her eyes, but she didn't open them. Instead, she drifted into a restless sleep, with the ghosts of her past making an appearance, mocking her while carrying a bundle far out of her reach.

When Tuva woke again, the light in the room signaled it was midday and this time, she was alone. Lifting her gown high, Tuva ran her fingers along her stomach and winced when she brushed against her scar. Setting the gown right, she crawled out of bed, clinging to it until her dizziness passed.

It didn't take long for Tuva to realize she was too weak to change out of her nightgown, so she grabbed her robe and clumsily tied the sash around her waist, careful not to bump her wound. She gathered her hair, tied it with a ribbon, and slowly made her way to the living area. When she walked into the room, all eyes turned to her, while Isak jumped up to come to her aid.

"I'm okay," Tuva said, "Just a little weak and sore."

Isak helped Tuva to the nearest chair. Once she was settled, he went toward the kitchen, muttering he would get her some water. Tuva watched her husband, and it wasn't lost on her that he was trying to hide his pain. She started to say something to try to reassure him, but changed her mind, and fumbled with the ribbon in her hair instead.

"Are you in pain?" Marriam asked.

"I'm sore, yes," Tuva said. "But I'm okay."

"You will regain your strength, and your pain will leave," Minwaadizi said.

"My friend, how did you come to be here?" Tuva asked.

"You came to me in a dream. You were surrounded by a pool of blood, and you told me you were dying," Minwaadizi said. "I told Makwa of my dream, and we came at once. I worried I was too late."

"We would have lost you, my Tuva," Isak said. "We almost did, but Minwaadizi saved you."

"And," Tuva paused, took a deep breath. "And the baby?"

"She was a beautiful baby girl," Isak said, setting the glass of water next to Tuva. He grabbed a chair and moved it to sit close to her.

"She was like the willow," Minwaadizi said. "She was too weak to make it through the storm."

"What happened to her?" Tuva asked.

A knock at the door interrupted Isak's attempt at a response and Marriam went to answer it. Marcy stood with a bouquet of fall flowers and a basket filled with food.

"Is she awake?" Marcy asked.

"I'm awake," Tuva called.

Marriam let Marcy in, shutting the door behind her.

"We were just talking about what happened," Isak said.

"Should I leave?" Marcy asked.

"No, it's okay," Tuva said. "Thank you so much for coming."

Marcy settled by Minwaadizi and asked, "How are you feeling?"

"I'm sore and a little weak, but okay," Tuva said. She turned toward Isak and asked a second time, "What happened to her?"

Isak gathered both of Tuva's hands in his. "She got stuck. She wouldn't come out. And you were losing so much blood. You almost stopped breathing a couple of times. So Minwaadizi pulled out a knife and started to slice your stomach open."

"Isak hollered for her to stop, but she didn't," Marriam interjected.

"Yeah, me and Marriam were struggling to hold him back," Marcy said. "I yelled for Spencer to come help, and him and Makwa came in. Even they struggled to hold him back."

"There was so much commotion and screaming. I'm so impressed at Minwaadizi being able to do what she did under such stressful circumstances," Marriam said.

"Yes, I kind of lost it," Isak said.

"Was she just not breathing when she came out?" Tuva asked.

"The cord was wrapped around her neck," Isak said. "She was so blue. Minwaadizi tried to revive her, but it was just not possible. We think she was already gone and that is why you went into labor when you did."

"I almost died?" Tuva whispered.

"Yes." Isak's voice broke.

"Minwaadizi brought you back to us, my daughter," Marriam said. "You slept for several days, but you were brought back to us.

Tuva's eyes settled on Minwaadizi. "My dear friend. To come to me at such a time."

"We are connected you and I," Minwaadizi said.

"Yes. Yes, we are," Tuva agreed, "and we always will be."

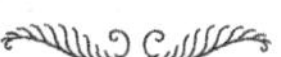

The water rushed over Tuva's back as Marriam rinsed her hair. A memory of another bath Marriam helped her with flitted through her mind and a shiver ran up Tuva's spine. The pain Tuva experienced made it feel like it had occurred yesterday instead of years ago.

"Are you cold?" Marriam asked.

"No, just memories," Tuva said.

"I didn't want to say anything, but I had the same thought," Marriam said.

"Such hardships we have faced together," Tuva said softly.

"Your hair is done. Would you like to soak a little?" Marriam asked.

"No, I want to get out. I'm looking forward to getting out of the cabin for once," Tuva said.

"Let me grab you a towel then," Marriam said.

Tuva closed her eyes and soaked up the last few seconds of warm water before Marriam returned and helped her stand.

"Your wound looks like it is healing well," Marriam said.

"Which one?" Tuva asked.

Marriam wrapped the towel around Tuva's shoulders, squeezed, and let go. "Some wounds take longer to heal. Give it time."

"I will try," Tuva said, and started drying off.

Marriam gave Tuva space but didn't go far just in case she needed help. Once Tuva was dressed, Marriam hollered for Isak to come take care of the bath. Tuva put her coat on and wrapped her shawl around her arms and explained she was desperate to get outside and near the water, but wanted to walk alone.

Isak tried to stop her, but Marriam cut him off, explaining Tuva needed this. Tuva thanked them for understanding and left the cabin. Walking to the point first, Tuva stared out at the gray of the water.

"You are matching my mood today, gichi-gami," Tuva whispered in the breeze.

A wave splashed against the rocks below as if in response to Tuva's comment, and she giggled. The sound startled her, as it had been weeks since she had laughed. Tuva studied the clouds in the distance and wondered if they would get snow before the end of the day.

Deciding she wanted to walk more, Tuva left the point and walked along the ridge down to the water's edge. She picked up a couple of rocks and tossed them into the cool water, and tried not to think about what had happened. She still felt raw and dead inside, and she wondered if she would ever feel alive again.

Tuva was so focused on her thoughts, she didn't realize anyone was approaching until Minwaadizi was standing next to her. At first, she wanted to be left alone, but Minwaadizi didn't say anything, so Tuva let it go.

They stood for several minutes before Tuva asked, "Aren't you going to ask me how I'm doing?"

"When you are ready to talk, I will listen," Minwaadizi said. "Until then, we will sit in silence."

Tuva nodded and turned back to the lake. The wind started to pick up as Tuva focused on the white flakes falling at the edge of the bay. Picking up a rock, Tuva threw it as far as she could. She started to throw a second one but stopped and dropped it at her feet.

"Lashing out at the lake won't change things," Minwaadizi said.

"I thought we were going to sit in silence until I'm ready to talk."

"Yes, but throwing rocks in anger is not sitting in silence."

"Will I ever be able to not feel so dead and empty?" Tuva asked.

"Losing a child is the worst kind of pain," Minwaadizi said.

"This happened to you," Tuva said, realizing her friend spoke from experience. "I'm sorry I was not there to help you."

"It happened before I knew you," Minwaadizi said. "I, like you, thought I would be empty forever. Then I saw a white woman smile at me on a road and something started to heal."

Tuva's lips curled slightly at the mention of their first meeting.

"Your friendship helped me come back to life," Minwaadizi continued. "We tried for more children and just when I thought I would never have a child again, I had my son."

"Is he here with you?"

"No, he is with our family," Minwaadizi said. "One day, our children will play together."

"I don't have any children," Tuva said with anguish.

"But you will when the time is right," Minwaadizi said.

"Perhaps," Tuva said.

"There will be a day you don't feel so empty and dead inside," Minwaadizi said.

"Isak and I talked about it, and we decided to have a little service for our baby. I know you and Makwa need to leave soon, but could you stay one more day?"

"We agreed to stay until I knew you would be okay," Minwaadizi said. "We will stay one more day."

Tuva linked arms with her friend, and they walked back toward the cabin. The snow never came to shore, but it stayed gray for the rest of the day. The following morning dawned with a bright sun and not a single cloud in the sky.

Nerves coursed through Tuva at the thought of everyone gathering over the small grave, but she was happy they were having a service for the baby. She donned her favorite dress, with an extra layer of undergarments, for although the sun was out, the weather was changing, and the air was cold.

Shortly after breakfast, everyone met at the tiny grave where Isak had erected a stone. He had promised Tuva he would carve whatever she wanted on it. The group sang a few songs of love and hope, and Isak shared a few words before turning it over to Tuva.

"I never thought we would be gathered here today," Tuva said, "standing over my precious baby's body buried beneath the ground. It makes me sad that I never got to hold her, but that sadness fades a little knowing her daddy was. Knowing he cared for her at the end eases some of the heartache."

Tuva had to pause to swallow the lump in her throat before she continued, "Isak and I talked for a long time about what we should name her or if we should name her. In the end, I told him only one name would do. Willow."

Chapter Thirty-Six

Dear Nora,

Winter hit us hard this year, but spring is finally here.

I wasn't sure if I would ever be able to write about this. My baby died. I almost died. My friend saved me. But sometimes I wish I would have died with the baby.

We haven't heard from Wally or Adam lately. We are hoping it's just because mail is slower in the winter, and that we will hear something soon.

Give Mamma and Pappa my love.

Tuva

P.S. We named her Willow.

Chapter Thirty-Seven

The soil felt good between Tuva's fingers as she worked in the garden. Tiny sprouts of green were popping up, and she was happy she'd started the seeds in the cabin when she had. She tried to put the conversation she had with Isak the night before out of her mind, but it kept plaguing her thoughts.

They hadn't made love since she had lost the baby and he wanted desperately for them to work together on getting past this. But Tuva couldn't reconcile herself to be happy after such devastation. She had said some awful things to him. He gently reminded her that she was not the only one who lost a child before stomping out of the cabin and slamming the door behind him.

Tuva wanted to fix things but didn't know how, so she chose to start work early in the garden instead of facing Isak and mending things. Standing to stretch her back and arms, Tuva noticed Marcy walking toward her with a bit of trepidation.

"Good morning," Tuva said.

Marcy's expression changed to joy. "Good morning. It's such a beautiful day."

"Yes, that it is," Tuva said.

"I was curious if you needed any help in the garden today?" Marcy asked.

"I think I'm okay today. Besides, I'm enjoying my solitude," Tuva said.

"Well. Um. Okay, then." Marcy started to leave, stopped, turned toward Tuva. "Do you mind if I ask you something?

"Sure," Tuva said.

"Are you ever going to let me help you in the garden?" Marcy asked. "It's just, you had told me that you would let me help you, especially since Marriam was focusing on other things now, but so far you haven't let me help at all."

"Well, I haven't needed any help," Tuva snapped.

Tears welled up in Marcy's eyes, and Tuva's stomach rolled. Marcy turned and ran away. Tuva tried to stop her, but Marcy just kept going. Tuva looked out at the water and felt her own tears spring to life.

"Who have I become?" she whispered into the breeze.

She followed Marcy and caught up with her as she was about to enter her cabin.

"Wait, Marcy. Wait, please," Tuva called.

Marcy paused, wiped at her eyes, and waited.

Tuva took a moment to catch her breath. "I'm so sorry, Marcy."

"I don't know what to say to that, Tuva," Marcy said. "This is the first time you have apologized to me."

"I have snapped at you before?"

"I know you are grieving, and that it can take a while to heal a broken heart," Marcy said.

"True, but that doesn't mean I get to lash out at everyone around me," Tuva said. She looked toward the direction of her cabin. "I have been snapping at Isak, too. I don't like how I have been acting, but I don't know how to fix it."

"I remember when I first heard about you," Marcy said. "Everyone in our little circle talked about this amazingly strong but kind woman. I was so scared to meet you, and I was so intimated by you. And I wondered if you would like me. But you opened your bay with open arms. You shared meals and stories with me, and you offered friendship instantly. I still see that in you."

Tuva wiped at the moisture on her face. "How could you see that?"

"Because even though you hurt and snap, you also put baskets on my porch filled with biscuits and bread and jam, and even leave notes with kind words."

"How do you know it wasn't from Marriam?" Tuva asked.

"Because I recognize the work you do," Marcy said.

"I'm so afraid to feel again, Marcy."

Marcy took a step toward Tuva, looked out at the water, then back at Tuva. "You told me once that it's the fear of the unknown that heightens those bad feelings. And that if we let it, that fear will lead us to making decisions we regret, or it will lead us to focus on the wrong things. And then you told me that the focus should be on those things we have to be grateful for."

Marcy paused. "That doesn't mean you have to forget her. But as you work on healing instead of focusing on your fear, try to focus on your husband and this beautiful bay. And that beautiful blue water."

Tuva's shoulders slumped forward, and she sat on the porch steps. She tried to choke back the emotions rising in the back of her throat. Marcy sat next to her and put her arm around her shoulder.

"Let it out, my friend," Marcy said. "My mamma used to tell me that sometimes what the heart needs is a really good cry."

Tuva let the dam break and she poured out her sorrows. Marcy held on and occasionally murmured encouragements, but mostly sat quietly, which allowed Tuva to just feel what she needed to. As Tuva regained her composure, she sat up, breathing in deeply. She was spent but a little lighter.

She turned her head to look at Marcy and thank her, but Tuva paused. Isak stood only a few feet away. She had no idea how long he had been there, but by the look on his face, she knew it had been long enough. Tuva stood, squeezed her friend's hand, and thanked her before walking toward Isak.

Stopping only inches from her husband, Tuva whispered, "I'm sorry, my Isak."

"My Tuva," Isak murmured. He encompassed her in his arms and kissed her gently on the mouth. "I love you so much."

"And I love you."

"We can get through this together," Isak said. "If you would let us ... get through it ... together."

"You're using my words against me," Tuva teased.

"Not against you," Isak said, as the corner of his mouth lifted. "I just remember them as wise words that I needed to hear one time."

"I suddenly have a need to run back to the cabin," Tuva said with a giggle.

"May I join you?"

"I was hoping you would," Tuva said with glee. She swatted Isak on the bottom and took off running toward the ridge.

"Tuva, in front of other people," Isak admonished.

"I doubt she cares," Tuva hollered. "Meet you in the bedroom."

Isak caught up with Tuva and smacked her behind as he ran past her. Tuva started laughing harder, making it difficult for her to breathe while she ran. She had to slow to a walk, and Isak came back to fall in step with her.

"It's so wonderful to hear that laugh of yours," Isak said.

"It is wonderful to laugh," Tuva said. "The ache is still there, but it is getting better."

"Of course it is still there, and it will most likely be there for a long time," Isak said. "The ache is still in my heart, too. Especially since it felt like I lost both of you that night."

Tuva stopped walking. "I'm sorry for pushing you away."

Isak turned to face Tuva. "You could never push me so far away that I wouldn't come running back to you."

Tuva lunged at her husband, pulling his mouth toward hers. Heat ignited between them and grew until Tuva had to pull away to catch her breath. "I suddenly need you, my Isak."

Isak grabbed her hand, and they continued their journey to the cabin. When they got on the porch, Isak swept her up in his arms and ran inside the house, slamming the door behind him. Once in their room, he lowered her gently to the bed, and a faint memory flickered in Tuva's mind of their first night together as husband and wife.

Chapter Thirty-Eight

Tuva stretched her arms and yawned. She had spent the rest of the morning in bed with her husband with a small respite of a light lunch, which they ate cuddled together between the sheets.

"I suppose we should face the rest of the day," Tuva said.

"My work can wait until tomorrow," Isak said, his fingers gliding on Tuva's arm.

"Yes, well, I promised your mother that I would go visit her this afternoon and I'm already late," Tuva said.

"I'm sure she'll understand your tardiness if you explain," Isak said.

"You're probably right," Tuva said, "but sometimes I like to keep our intimacies between you and me."

"Ha. This from the woman who swatted her husband's butt in front of our neighbor," Isak said.

Tuva planted a kiss on her husband's mouth before rolling off the bed to tidy herself and get dressed. If it wasn't for needing to make amends with her mother-in-law too, she would have stayed in bed.

"I would feel better if I met with Mamma," she said. "I need to apologize to her, too, I think."

"If that would make you feel better."

"Yes, it would. Besides, we can pick up where we left off later tonight."

Isak came up behind her and kissed the back of her neck.

A shiver went through her body. "Goodness, keep doing that, and I may have to take my dress back off."

"Don't tempt me," Isak said as he got dressed.

Tuva finished buttoning her dress and kissed her husband on the cheek. "See you later, at dinner."

"I'm looking forward to it."

Tuva left to go meet Marriam, and she tried to think of what she would say to apologize when Marriam rounded the corner in the path. Tuva beamed at the sight of her.

"I was just heading your way," Tuva said.

"I was coming to you. I thought perhaps in my old age I had forgotten what we agreed upon," Marriam said, studying Tuva closely.

Tuva hugged Marriam. "I'm sorry for anything I have done the last couple of months that may have hurt you or Josef."

When they pulled apart, Marriam clasped Tuva's hands in hers. "Oh, my daughter. You have been carrying the weight of a heavy sorrow around with you. I didn't take offense at any remark or slight. I know what it is to grieve. I don't know what it is to lose a child and I pray this war doesn't give me that type of grief, but I do know what it is to be surrounded by it."

"Ever the loving mother."

"Ever the loving daughter."

Isak left the cabin, and Tuva caught sight of him. Her cheeks started to burn, and she tried to hide her face.

"So, I see you have made up with my son as well," Marriam said.

Tuva giggled and looked down at the ground. When she looked back up toward Isak, something caught her attention on the water. It was hard to make it out through the trees, and she squinted.

"What is it?" Marriam asked.

"I don't know," Tuva said. "I thought I saw a boat, but the trees are in the way, so now I don't know if maybe I'm seeing things."

"Let's go look," Marriam said.

Tuva linked arms with her mother-in-law. They talked about the garden as they started their descent down the ridge, and Tuva realized everyone else in the bay had gathered at the shoreline. She hadn't been seeing things. A boat was about to dock.

"I wonder who this could be?" Tuva asked. Her heart started to pound, and her stomach turned over, thinking it could be unwanted information about Wally or Adam.

"You don't suppose it could be, you know, news about something?" Marriam asked, stumbling over her words.

"I had the same thought, but let's do what we know how to do best," Tuva said, trying to reassure Marriam.

"And what is that?" Marriam asked.

"What is it you tell me? Cling to hope," Tuva said.

The vessel was made secure, and several people started to disembark. A woman all but leaped onto the dock and said something to Isak. When he pointed in Tuva's direction, a flash of recognition flitted across her face, and she started moving quickly toward Tuva.

Tuva paused and squinted to get a better look. A loud screech escaped her lips, and she took off running.

"Tuva, what is it?" Marriam asked, trying to keep up.

But Tuva couldn't respond. She was laughing, crying, and running as fast as she could. She hoped she wouldn't trip and fall, but the woman running toward her spurred her on. Tuva ran headlong into the woman's arms.

"Nora!"

"Tuva!"

The sisters held each other, repeating the other's name. Tuva let the tears flow freely while she surveyed the dock behind them. She noticed a man with two little girls huddled against him.

Tuva pulled away to study her sister's face. "How are you here?"

"I'm here because you are, big sister," Nora said. "It's a long story, and I will explain it all to you. But first you need to come meet my husband and my little girls."

"You have babies?" Tuva asked.

Nora stopped and grabbed her sister's hands. "I received the letter about Willow right before we sailed. I'm sorry if meeting them pains you."

"On the contrary," Tuva said. "You have no idea how much joy it brings my heart to meet them and to see you."

The sisters linked arms and started walking toward the dock when Tuva remembered Marriam. She turned to her mother-in-law and started to apologize for running off. But Marriam waved her hand at Tuva, reassuring her to go on.

Nora gushed about their trip and how it wasn't nearly as exciting of a boat trip as Tuva's had been. She talked about seeing the evidence of the war and the train ride being challenging at times. But how the worst part of the trip was the wagon ride from the cities.

Tuva chuckled and couldn't stop watching her sister explain her trip here. She glanced at Isak, who was beaming at her, but she looked back toward the dock when he nodded in its direction. Tuva stopped and Nora followed suit.

"Can you believe it?" Nora whispered.

"Mamma," Tuva said, and ran to her mother's waiting arms.

More laughter and tears escaped from Tuva and just when she thought her heart would burst, she noticed her father hanging back a few steps, ringing his hat in his hand. Tuva pulled away from her mother and walked slowly to him.

"I don't even know what to say right now," Tuva said.

"I never thought I would see you again," her father said, watching her warily.

"And I you, Pappa," she said. She wanted to hug him so badly. She said a silent prayer he would accept her affection.

But her fears were laid to rest quickly when he held his arms wide. "I have missed you, daughter."

Chapter Thirty-Nine

Setting the last of the dishes out, Tuva called everyone to dinner. They were going to have a buffet since there were so many joining them. Marcy and Spencer had tried to excuse themselves, as they didn't want to interfere with the family reunion, but Tuva wouldn't hear of it.

Everyone gathered and the group started to move through the line. Tuva prepared her plate and sat at the table with the rest of the women along with her little nieces, Ingrid and Carina.

"How old are your girls?" Marriam asked.

"Ingrid is the oldest at four years, and Carina is two," Nora said.

"They are just lovely, and I love their names," Marriam said, glancing at Tuva.

"Thank you," Nora said. "Ingrid was named after Tobias' eldest sister, who passed when she was a child. And Carina was named for me and Tuva's grandmother. I always loved her name."

"That is a beautiful tribute," Marcy said. "We hope one day our little bundle will be named for someone we love."

"Your little bundle?" Tuva questioned. As much as she wanted to be excited for her friend, she couldn't help but feel the ache of her loss.

"Oh, Tuva," Marcy said, "I didn't mean for that to slip out. Yes, I'm pregnant and am due at Christmas."

"This is great news," Tuva said, attempting to hide her pain.

"We can talk of something else," Marcy said.

"No. Life goes on. And I'm okay," Tuva said, trying to convince herself this was true.

"You don't look okay, Tuva," Nora said.

"I will be," Tuva said.

"It's okay if you're not," Tuva's mother, Elin, said.

"I know," Tuva said, placing her hands in her lap and staring at them.

Marriam went to Tuva and hugged her. "Come help with checking the food."

Tuva followed her mother-in-law into the kitchen, where they perused the dishes and refilled bowls. Marriam stopped Tuva from returning to the table. "We can take a walk if you need to."

"No," Tuva said. "As much as I still have pain, I have to keep putting one foot in front of the other."

Marriam caressed her cheek. "My strong daughter."

Tuva squeezed her hand. "Thank you for recognizing that I needed a minute to collect myself, and stepping in to make sure I took it."

"Your mamma is here now, but that doesn't mean I will stop being your mamma."

Hugging Marriam, Tuva took a deep breath. "Okay, we should go back to the others."

When Tuva returned to the table, her mamma asked, "Can I help with anything?"

"No, Mamma. I'm okay. And the food is ready for anyone who wants to get more," Tuva said.

"Well, let me know how I can help in the future," her mamma said, fumbling with her napkin.

Tuva nodded and focused on finishing her meal. As excited as she was to have her family here, she knew there would be adjustments. They were going to need to get to know each other again, and she was anxious on how it was going to go.

"What are your thoughts on sleeping arrangements, Tuva?" Marriam asked.

"My thought was that Mamma and Pappa could sleep in our spare room and then Nora and her family could sleep in the loft," Tuva said.

"That's a lot of people under one roof," Marriam said.

"Wouldn't be the first time," Tuva said with a laugh.

"How about your parents come stay with us?" Marriam offered.

"That is so generous of you," Tuva said.

"Yes, and then Nora's family could stay here," Marriam suggested.

"That would work just fine for us," Tuva's mother said.

"Well, I guess it's settled then," Tuva said.

The rest of dinner, the women discussed more details of their journey to Minnesota until it was time to clean up. Marriam and Marcy offered to do the cleaning so Tuva could spend time with her sister and mother. Tuva took them up on their offer and suggested they walk around outside a bit.

The sisters walked, swinging Carina in between them while their mother walked along chatting with Ingrid. The conversation was light until Tuva asked a question from earlier in the day.

"How is it that you are here?"

Nora glanced back at their mother, and Tuva noticed they exchanged a look and when her mother nodded, Nora said, "We almost lost Mamma."

"What?" Tuva asked.

"Please let me share," Nora said. "We almost lost Mamma. Do you remember my letter explaining she had been sick? What I didn't share is that her illness returned and that time we almost lost her. Father was beside himself. Tobias and I helped as much as we could, but we lived too far away."

"How scary for you all," Tuva said.

"It was a scary time," Nora said. "But Mamma started to mend, and one day Father blurted out he couldn't stand the whole family being scattered all over the world."

"I was so shocked because you know how your father can be," their mother jumped in.

"Reserved. Unkind. Cool," Tuva said.

"That's a bit harsh, Tuva," her mother said.

"Is it? He was rarely kind to me," Tuva said.

"Your father loves you girls. He was just brought up in a home where the man provided. The man led. The man took care of the needs of his family. But the man was not to show emotion or weakness," her mamma said.

"I will say he does seem different now," Tuva said.

"He is different," Nora said. "When Mamma got sick, he was terrified of losing her. And he told me later that he realized he had made a mistake in not sharing his love for her and for us."

"He was afraid of showing love because he thought it meant he was a weak man and his father enforced being a strong man, sometimes rather harshly," their mother said.

"Give him some time," Nora said. "He will eventually talk with you about it. I know he will."

"How do you know?" Tuva asked.

"Because he talked to me about it," Nora said.

"This conversation encourages my heart, but it still doesn't explain how you are here," Tuva said, smiling down at her niece as she swung her in the air again.

"Things got really hard at home," their mother said.

"Yes," Nora said. "It was becoming increasingly difficult to find food with the famine. Pappa decided to sell the farm and move in with us when he struggled to make ends meet. That was a hard blow for him, but he took it much better than he would have years ago."

"Your sister was living in the city and Tobias had a decent job," her mamma said, "but we knew it wouldn't be long before having too many mouths to feed would take a toll on us."

"It was my idea to come here," Nora said.

"Even after all the hardships I wrote about?" Tuva asked.

"I figured hardships faced as a family would be better than hardships faced alone," Nora said.

"That is my way of thinking, too," Tuva said.

"It took a while for us to get everything in place," their mother said.

"Yes, but when we did, we decided to surprise you," Nora said.

"Best surprise. Best gift, ever," Tuva said. She swung down and picked up her niece, giggling, while she spun her around.

"Tuva, I know your Pappa will be asking you this, but I wanted to make sure it's okay for us to ask," her mother said.

Tuva stopped spinning her niece and asked, "What question would that be?"

"Would it be okay if we built our homes here?" Nora asked.

"Of course," Tuva said. "We have plenty of land for family to join us here."

Nora hugged Tuva and said, "I knew this was the best decision for us."

"Sharing this place with you would be an honor," Tuva said.

The sisters pulled apart. Nora looked past Tuva and gasped. "Mamma, have you ever seen anything more beautiful in all your life?"

"This place is quite stunning," their mother said.

Tuva grinned at her family, thankful they were there and thankful they loved her bay as she did. The women walked back toward the cabin while they talked about Tuva's garden and the delicious dinner they had. As they neared the men, a hush fell over the group, and Tuva exchanged a look with Isak, which spoke of excitement.

Marriam and Marcy joined the crowd, and Marcy suggested her and Spencer head home. Once they left, Marriam indicated she was going to go prepare the cabin for Elin and Loui to stay. Elin offered to come help and Nora decided to get the girls settled for the night.

"Did you gentlemen have a nice visit?" Tuva asked.

"Yes, your sister's husband, Mr. Lundin, was just telling us that he too has a knack with woodworking, but his heart really lies in fishing," Josef shared.

"Please, call me Tobias. And yes, fishing was what my grandfather did, and I always wanted to follow in his footsteps," Tobias said.

"That sounds lovely," Tuva said. "We could use a fisherman."

Tuva couldn't help but notice her father was studying her intently, and she thought about pulling him aside to talk with him now. She wrestled with what to do for several minutes, but decided against it. Although Nora had said he had changed, past actions from him deterred her, and she decided to go see if Nora needed assistance instead.

Excusing herself, Tuva made her way into the cabin. As she shut the door, she overheard Isak say, "She will forgive you, Loui. Tuva has the biggest heart out of any person I know."

When Tuva found Nora, she realized her sister had been crying.

"Nora, what is it?" Tuva asked.

"I'm just happy to be here," Nora said. "The trip over was so long and we had such difficulties traveling up here with the war going on. And, well, I'm so tired and don't feel the greatest."

"Are you sick?" Tuva asked.

Nora studied her hands. "I'm pregnant."

Tuva sat down on the bed and looked out the window. *It's not fair.* She tried to push the thought out of her head and picked up a blanket to distract her.

"I know it must seem like it is so unfair," Nora said.

"You are reading my mind," Tuva said.

"Only because you tend to send your thoughts into the world for all to hear," Nora said.

"Marriam says I'm like an open book."

"Just means you're honest."

"Ha, Marriam says the same thing, too," Tuva said.

Nora hugged Tuva, and whispered, "I so love you, sister, and I'm so sorry for your pain and for your precious Willow."

Tuva leaned into her sister and closed her eyes. "I love you too."

"Mamma, where are we sleeping?" Ingrid asked.

Tuva pulled away and said, "Ah, now little one, you get to sleep in the best spot in the house. In the loft. In fact, how about you come with me, and you can help me get you and your sister's bed ready while your mamma helps Carina get ready for bed."

Ingrid held Tuva's hand, and they went upstairs. It didn't take long to finish, and Nora was upstairs, Carina in tow. The sisters got the girls down for the night and went back to the kitchen table to chat until Isak and Tobias came in.

Tuva was looking past Isak for her father when Isak said, "He left with Josef. But we will see them in the morning."

Trying to smile, Tuva nodded, but wasn't sure how to feel after everything her mother and Nora had shared. Isak squeezed her hand and sat down next to her. The two couples chatted for a little while until Isak suggested they all turn in for the night.

When they were alone, Tuva could tell Isak was studying her, and she fidgeted with the front of her dress, trying to undo the buttons.

"Need some help with that?" Isak gently asked.

"No, I can manage if my hands would stop shaking," Tuva said.

"Are you nervous?"

"I'm just so overwhelmed with all that has happened today that I'm a bit jittery," Tuva said.

"That is to be expected," Isak said. "Perhaps we should pick up where we left off earlier today. Maybe it would help you feel better."

Tuva smirked at her husband's goofy grin. "As much as your suggestion is enticing, I must pass. I'm not sure how I feel about making love to my husband while my sister tries to sleep in the next room."

It was Isak's turn to laugh before saying, "Wow, I can't believe they are here."

"Neither can I."

"Do you think they will stay here for good?"

"Mamma and Nora said Pappa is going to ask if they can build here."

"Your father and Tobias hinted as much," he said, "but I think your father wants to talk with you first."

"Why do you say that?" Tuva asked.

"Because your father said he was hesitant about committing to anything until he had the right conversation with the right person," Isak said.

"I don't know what to think about this, well, this new man that my Pappa apparently is," Tuva said.

"Give him a chance to share his story, Tuva," Isak encouraged.

"I will. I grew up, and then left Sweden with this idea of a man that was distant and cold. And now here he is in my little bay, and he is supposedly reformed and new. I just don't know," Tuva said, shaking her head.

"See what he has to say," Isak said.

"I will." Tuva grew quiet as she climbed into bed.

"Are you okay? Besides the situation with your father, I mean. You seem upset about something," Isak probed.

"Marcy is pregnant, and so is Nora," Tuva said. "I know we haven't even tried again, but the sting of losing Willow is still so piercing. I want to be happy for them. And I do feel happy for them. But—"

"But you also feel sad," he interrupted.

"Yes."

"It's okay to feel happy for them, and also feel sad, my Tuva. It's the power of and."

"I know. I just. Um. I don't know."

"Yes, I agree," Isak said.

"Are you okay?" she asked.

"I will be," he said, "because you and I will go through this next step together and we will go through the next hard step together, too."

"I've missed us," Tuva said.

"I've missed us, too," Isak agreed.

"Maybe if we are quiet ..."

"You don't need to say anything more," Isak said, reaching for her.

Chapter Forty

Dearest Wally,

I'm not sure if you received my letters about my family coming here. I'm not even sure if you and Adam are still alive. It's been weeks since we heard about Gettysburg. We need to know if you both are okay. And if it isn't too much trouble, let us also know about Bill.

Your loving sister,

Tuva

P.S. I haven't told anyone else yet. I'm pregnant.

Chapter Forty-One

Isak read the telegram while Tuva studied her husband intently. She knew it wasn't good news and held her breath, waiting for him to look at her. He lowered the paper slowly and looked out at the water.

"You're scaring me," she said, grabbing her husband's hand.

"We need to gather Mamma and Pappa at once."

"Is it bad?"

Isak didn't say anything and started to walk toward the ridge. Tuva felt the blood drain from her face and followed her husband. She tried several times to get Isak's attention, to no avail. Finally, Tuva stopped in the middle of the path in front of Isak.

"Please, just tell me something," Tuva begged.

Isak clasped his wife's hand gently. "Tuva, I want to share all of this when we are together, but I will say it isn't the best of news."

"Oh, Isak," Tuva screeched. "Are they dead?"

"Please, Tuva."

"You're right," Tuva said, shaking her head, while moisture formed in the corners of her eyes. "It's important for your mother and father to be present."

Tuva followed close behind Isak the rest of the way. She refused to let her mind wander, but she was terrified of the news. When they reached Josef and Marriam's home, bile rose, and she had to stop to be sick.

Isak went to Tuva's side. "I haven't even told you anything yet."

"I'm just a bit nauseous already today and this just pushed my stomach over the edge, I think," Tuva said, wiping her mouth with a handkerchief.

Studying his wife closely, Isak asked, "Tuva, should I be worried about you? Are you sick?"

Tuva weakly lifted the corners of her mouth. "I was hoping to share this later, but no, I'm not sick."

"Are you pregnant?"

Tuva nodded, hating that he was finding out right before having to share whatever bad news he was carrying.

Isak gathered her into his arms and whispered, "This makes my load lighter, my Tuva. Thank you for telling me this now."

"Are you sure?" she asked. "I wanted this to be shared during different circumstances."

"No, this is perfect timing," Isak said. He squeezed her a little tighter before letting her go. Tuva linked her arm with her husband's while he turned toward his mission, and they went up the steps of his parent's porch together.

Isak lifted his hand to knock when the door flew open.

"Gracious, Tuva," Marriam said, as she walked out the door. "Are you okay? I saw you get sick on the path. Do you by chance have some news for us?"

Tuva nodded, but instead of smiling, she struggled to keep from crying.

"What is it?" Josef asked from behind Marriam.

"We need to talk," Isak said. "We received some news."

"Come, let's go inside then," Marriam said, her face growing pale.

Marriam insisted Tuva's parents stay in the room, but not wanting to intrude, they sat by the fireplace, while the rest of them settled around the kitchen table. Once everyone was seated, Isak unfolded the paper he carried.

"It says here that Adam was injured, and at a hospital recovering, but—" Isak started.

"But what?" Tuva asked.

"Wally is missing."

"What does that mean?" Marriam asked.

"I'm not sure yet, Mamma," Isak said. "The battle was a difficult one—we all know that. I'm sure they are trying to identify all the wounded and killed as fast as they can."

"It's been weeks, though," Tuva said. "Surely they can identify people quicker than that."

"We have to remember, some men are being treated by the opposition," Isak said.

"I suppose that could be the case," Tuva said. "I hope that doesn't mean they won't get the treatment they need."

"I hope not either," Isak said.

"What of Adam's injuries?" Marriam asked.

"It doesn't say much other than he should be able to come home soon," Isak said. He looked down at the paper, and when he looked back at Tuva, pain crossed his face.

"Isak, what is it?" Marriam asked.

Isak reached across the table and held Tuva's hand. "Tuva, I ..." he stopped and started again, "Tuva, I don't know how to say this."

"Isak, you're scaring me again."

"Honey, what is it?" Marriam asked. "If there is more information, please share it."

Isak paused, and Tuva tried to figure out why he was being so cryptic. The blood drained from her cheeks as realization dawned on her.

"Bill," Tuva whispered, looking down at her hands.

"That's right. He didn't make it."

"Oh, Isak," Tuva said. She looked across the table at her husband, trying to hold back the emotions invading her, but she couldn't keep it inside. She buried her face in her hands.

"Who is Bill?" Tuva's mother asked from across the room.

"It's a long story," Marriam said, putting her arm around Tuva.

"He was a friend of mine, and a good friend to Tuva," Isak said, getting up from his chair, and going to his wife. He held her to him while she cried.

"Poor Wally and Adam," Tuva said in between sobs. "I'm just heartbroken for them. For all of us. And for Bill."

"And we wouldn't expect anything less," Marriam said, crying along with Tuva.

As the tears lessened and Tuva regained her composure, she squeezed Marriam's hand. "I'm so sorry for blubbering when I need to be the strong one for you."

"Oh, my sweet daughter, we are all sad and scared for your brothers, but we have hope," Marriam said.

Isak wiped the tears off Tuva's face. "And to lose someone you love is a different kind of heartache. I know, I know. It's different. But you did love him, and that's okay."

"I did. But I always loved you differently and so much more," Tuva said.

"I know, my Tuva. I know," Isak said.

Tuva didn't think it was possible to love her husband any more than she did in that moment. She knew he was sad about losing his friend too, but she was grateful he understood it was a deeper loss for her after their history.

Glancing over at her mother, Tuva realized she would have to explain Bill to her and dreaded the conversation.

Isak must have been reading her thoughts, for he stood up. "Elin, Loui, I'm sure this is confusing for you. Bill was a close friend of the family and we lost him in the war."

"I see," Tuva's mother said. "I'm saddened by your loss, and for the unfortunate news of your brothers, Isak. They will be in our thoughts in the coming days. What can we do now? How about some coffee? And I will prepare dinner tonight. You all need to rest after such brutal news."

Tuva slumped in her chair as the room started to spin. Isak had taken such care with breaking the news, but with her pregnancy hormones choosing to rage, Tuva needed a break. She knew it was better for her if she went home to lie down. She tried to stand and explain this, but the room twirled out of control, her knees buckled under her, and everything went dark.

"Tuva, can you hear me?" Isak's voice whispered in the distance.

Tuva could hear him say her name more urgently. She opened her eyes and found she was lying on Marriam's bed.

"Honey, are you okay?" her mother asked.

Tuva looked around and realized she was surrounded by both of her mothers and her husband.

"What happened?" she asked.

"You fainted, my dear," Marriam said. "So, I must ask again. Do you have something to tell us?"

"Some good news might be enjoyed about now," Isak said.

"I'm pregnant."

Chapter Forty-Two

Marcy handed Tuva a glass of water, then wiped her brow with the back of her hand. Tuva studied her friend over her glass and was thankful she had allowed her to help in the garden.

"Having your help today was so appreciated," Tuva said.

"I'm just thankful you are showing me the ropes," Marcy said. "Next year, Spencer and I want to have our own little garden. Nothing to rival yours, of course, but just a little something for us would be nice."

"I love that you want your own garden, and I would be happy to help you with it if you want or need it," Tuva said.

"That is so thoughtful. Thank you."

A child's squeal echoed from the ridge, and Tuva looked in that direction. Ingrid dashed in between the trees, followed closely by a laughing Nora.

"How is their house coming along? Marcy asked.

"It's getting there," Tuva said. "Once they are finished with that, they will start on my parents' home."

"Did your father ever talk with you?" Marcy asked.

"No, Mamma apparently told him that we had chatted, and that I said they could build here, so he hasn't attempted to talk with me yet."

"Do you think his nerves are getting the better of him?" Marcy asked.

"I suppose that could be it. Or he hasn't changed as much as they all like to claim he has," Tuva said.

"Don't discount him yet," Marcy said.

"They have been here for how long, and he hasn't said a word yet," Tuva said.

"Yes, well, may I remind you that you can be a bit intimidating at times. You are, after all, the strongest person I know," Marcy said.

"You really think he is struggling to talk to me?" Tuva said.

"Yes. Yes, I do," Marcy said.

"Isak says the same," Tuva said. Studying her friend, she asked, "How are you feeling?"

"I'm feeling good for the most part. Some morning sickness and a little tired, but I'm okay," Marcy said.

"I'm glad to hear it," Tuva said.

"Me and Spencer are going to head into Duluth next week so the doctor can check me over to make sure I'm doing okay," Marcy added.

"That is smart," Tuva said.

"Are you and Isak trying again?" Marcy asked, but followed quickly by saying, "Oh, I'm sorry. I know that is probably none of my business."

"You can ask me anything anytime, my friend," Tuva said with a mischievous grin. "Yes, and we have been successful."

"Oh, Tuva, this is wonderful news," Marcy said, but sobered when she looked past Tuva. "Um, looks like it might be time for that talk you have been waiting for."

"What?" Tuva asked, turning to see her father walking toward them with a strange look on his face.

"Go on. I will see you tomorrow," Marcy said.

"See you tomorrow," Tuva said, and walked toward her father. When she was only a few feet from him, she asked, "Pappa, is everything alright."

"Tuva, we need to talk," her father said.

"Okay, did I do something wrong?" Tuva asked.

"What?" her father asked. "Why would you think you did something wrong?"

"You seem upset," Tuva said.

"Oh, no. I'm just a little nervous and also determined. I have been putting this off because I have been too scared to face it," he said.

"Face what?"

"Face you. Face how I treated you." Her father paused and ran his hand through his hair. "Do you mind if we go sit down by the water?"

"Sure, that is fine with me," Tuva said.

Tuva described her favorite spot on the dock as they walked to it. Her father nodded, but didn't say anything until they were settled.

"I have made a lot of mistakes in my life, Tuva," he began.

"It's okay, Pappa," Tuva said. "We all have made mistakes in life."

"That is kind of you to say," he said, "but please let me say my piece."

"Okay."

"I grew up in a home where my father beat us if we showed any sentiments that seemed too feminine to him. His brother had loved to help their mother with sewing, and he had taken offense to that, as it embarrassed him. He swore he wouldn't have girly sons."

"Pappa, that is awful," Tuva said.

"Thank you for your kindness," he said. "I was never really taught that it was okay to show love. But when I met your mother, I fell so much in love with her. I married her, then had you, and I cried. I held you and I cried."

Tuva was stunned but didn't say anything.

"Instead of leaning into those feelings of love, I got scared," he continued. "I thought I had become weak and if my father saw me acting that way, well, I thought he would have been disappointed. That somehow, I had become less of a man."

"I hope you know that's not true."

"I know that now," he said, "but at the time, it scared me. So, I kept you at arm's length. But it never meant I loved you less. That day you left for here, Tuva, I almost broke down. It was the first time I struggled to keep my emotions in check in so long. It was why I turned away so quickly. I couldn't stand for you or anyone to see me as weak."

"You are not weak," she said.

"You, of course, are right," he said. "I know that the love I have for your mother and for you girls is what makes me strong. I know now that crying is just an outward expression of my love for you. And I know that my father was a foolish man."

"I'm so sorry I misjudged you, Pappa," Tuva said.

"You have nothing to apologize for, daughter," her father said.

Tuva took a step toward him, but years of rejection caused her to pause.

"When your mamma got sick, I was so scared. Then we almost lost her, and I broke down. I realized that I had also been a foolish man." He paused and ran his fingers through his hair. "Tuva, can you ever forgive me for being so cold and distant? I can't imagine what you must have thought. And for that, I will always be sorry. But I hope you can find it in your heart to forgive me and learn to love me, anyway."

Tuva held her father's face in her hands. "Pappa, know this. I have never not loved you. I have always loved you. And of course, I can forgive you. We all make mistakes. We are all human."

He hugged her, and when they pulled apart, she linked arms with his. She suggested they make their way back toward home. The conversation changed to a lighter tone, while a buried wound in Tuva's heart was healed.

Chapter Forty-Three

Glancing down the street, Tuva wondered when she might be here next. The days were growing colder and shorter. She and Isak had gone into Duluth for a couple of days, so she could see the doctor and he could get supplies. The doctor's visit had gone well, but due to her past pregnancy, he suggested she rest more, especially as time went on.

The bustle around her surprised Tuva. It amazed her how much Duluth had changed since she had first arrived with her husband. There was still no word about Wally. Thinking of him, Tuva frowned as she looked around, hoping to catch a glimpse of Isak. Adam had written several times, advising he was mending well, and he was working on finding out what happened to Wally.

"Excuse me, miss, but you look like you have lost something."

Tuva jumped at the voice behind her, but she quickly recognized it. She swung around to face its owner.

"Adam," Tuva screeched, and flung herself into her brother's arms. "Have you seen Isak?"

"So that is what you lost?" Adam said with a smirk.

"I'm happy to see that the battles you have faced did not quash your sense of humor."

"No," Adam said, "on the contrary. It reminded me how precious life really is."

Tuva realized they were not the only two standing there chatting.

"Please forgive my manners," Tuva said, extending her hand to the woman next to Adam. "I'm Tuva Nilsson, Adam's sister."

"Ah, yes, we are being rude," Adam said. "Tuva, this is Frances. My wife."

"Your wife?" Tuva said. She yanked her extended hand away and hugged the woman. "Well, in this family we hug, not shake hands. Welcome, Frances."

"Please, call me Franny," the woman said softly, hugging Tuva back. "It's truly an honor to meet you. Adam talks so much of the family and so much of you."

"All good I hope," Tuva said.

"Of course," Adam said, winking at her. "You are, after all, my hero, Tuva."

Tuva's cheeks warmed. "You are making me blush, Adam. But, oh it is so good that you are home. And such a pleasure to meet you, Franny. I can't wait to hear more about how you two met."

"Tuva, there you are," Isak said as he came up behind Adam and Franny.

Tuva watched her husband closely to see when he would realize who she was talking with. Adam turned around, and Isak howled. The brothers hugged, smacking each other's backs. When they pulled apart, Tuva made the introductions between Franny and Isak, and more hugs and laughter followed.

"When did you arrive?" Tuva asked.

"Just now," Franny said. "We were walking to find a place to stay for the night when we ran into you."

"Oh, well, we must walk to the hotel together. I'm sure they have more rooms available," Tuva said. "Then you can go the rest of the way with us tomorrow."

"Your timing couldn't have been more perfect," Isak said.

"So, you are heading back to the bay tomorrow, then?" Adam asked.

"Yes, we came into town to have Tuva see the doctor, and for us to get supplies."

"Tuva, does this mean what I think it means?" Adam asked.

"That it does," Tuva said.

"This is cause for a celebration," Adam said.

"No, the cause for celebration is you and your bride coming home," Tuva exclaimed.

"Do you have more bags than this small one?" Isak asked.

"We left the rest of our luggage down at the docks until we could get settled with arrangements for the night," Adam said. "I guess I should have looked closer—I might have found our boat."

"Well, let's get your accommodations set up for the night, then you and I can get what is needed for tonight, and secure everything else on our boat," Isak said.

"Yes, and then we will celebrate with a delicious meal at the hotel," Tuva said.

"Always thinking of your stomach these days," Isak said, cackling.

"Yes, that is what one thinks of when they are eating for two," Franny said.

"I had a feeling I would like you," Tuva said. "Thank you for sticking up for me."

"Us women have to stick together," Franny said.

"Indeed we do," Tuva said, linking arms with Franny. "Come, let's get you settled. You must be exhausted."

The group made their way to the hotel and got a room reserved. Tuva and Franny waited for their men in Tuva and Isak's room, and Tuva enjoyed the story of how Franny and Adam met. They continued to talk of lighter things until Tuva couldn't stand it any longer.

"Has there been no word?" Tuva asked.

"Of Wally?" Franny asked.

"Yes, of Wally."

"Adam has worked tirelessly," Franny said, "and I know he will want to share more when he gets back. But he has not given up. We were still waiting to hear about a few leads when he received the news that he was being released from medical care and was able to travel. He decided it was best to go home and requested for word to be sent there."

"Hopefully those leads will turn up something. Anything," Tuva said.

"The not knowing is almost unbearable, I know," Franny said. "We had a similar circumstance with my brother, who we found out didn't make it. But, when we finally learned the news, we were thankful to at least know. We could finally move forward."

"Yes, I suppose we feel somewhat the same about it," Tuva said.

"Tuva," Franny started, stopped and took a deep breath, then asked, "Could I ask you a question?"

"Uh, oh. Am I in trouble?" Tuva smiled, but her stomach flip-flopped, and she worried about the direction their conversation was heading.

"Sorry, I don't mean to sound so cryptic," Franny said.

"You can always ask me anything, Franny," Tuva said.

"Bill talked of you often. As though there was something between you," Franny hesitated again.

"You are wondering if I had an affair with him," Tuva said.

"Oh goodness. No, not that," Franny said. "Well, I guess maybe a little of that. But I wondered what it could have been since I could never get close to him. He and I met a few times, but he kept his distance, and said his heart belonged to another.

"Adam and I connected after that, but I always wondered if the other woman was you. Then, when Bill died, Adam didn't say much about it. I do think he has something for you from Bill, though."

Tuva was sure the color drained from her face. Her throat dried, and she went to get a glass of water. Taking a couple of big gulps, she relaxed.

Once she knew she could talk again, Tuva said, "Bill and I were brought together by a hardship that I will someday explain to you. He loved me. Very much, I'm finding."

"Everyone who knows you, loves you. That is what Adam and Wally always said."

"I'm not sure what to think about that," Tuva said.

"I would think it a high compliment," Franny said. "I just hope that one day someone could say the same of me."

"Are you sure they don't?" Tuva asked. "I would think Adam wouldn't have married you unless people could."

"You're so kind," Franny said, her cheeks turning pink. "And my apologies for asking such intimate questions that are surely none of my business."

Tuva waved her hand, let out a hoot, and said, "You are family. My new sister. As I said before, you can always ask me anything."

The door burst open, and Tuva jolted. She slammed her hand against her chest before crossing to greet Isak.

"You startled me."

"I see that," Isak said before kissing Tuva soundly. "Are you hungry and ready for dinner?"

"Starving," Tuva said.

Tuva could tell Isak read something on her face but was thankful he kept quiet about it. She knew he would ask her about it later. And she was right.

When they were crawling into bed later, Isak asked, "What happened with Franny while we were away?"

"She asked me about Bill," Tuva said quietly.

"Ah, I see. And what did you say?"

"I shared very little actually, but enough to suffice for now, I think," she said. "Sometimes I wonder if that ordeal or the memory of it will be with me forever."

"He played a large role in your life," Isak said. "It took me a while to realize that he provided a solace for you that you needed during a time when you were most vulnerable. It wasn't his fault he fell in love with you. And it wasn't your fault either. It just was."

"It still breaks my heart that we hurt you."

"It shouldn't," he said. "Life is funny how it works things out. When I read the telegram that day indicating that Bill had died, I knew that it would solidify your feelings for him. I knew you had never allowed yourself before that time to entertain the possibility of feelings for him because of your love for me. I knew then that you and I would always be. And it won't ever change my love for you. My only fear is the ghost of him being something that forever haunts us."

"I don't know what to say to that," she said.

"Say nothing for now," he said, wrapping his arms around her. He kissed her gently, but a fire ignited inside of her, and she could tell it was the same for Isak. Sleep would be delayed.

Chapter Forty-Four

They had just cast off when Franny leaned over the railing. Tuva watched her sister-in-law study the water before asking, "So, what do you think of our gichi-gami?"

"Your what?" Franny asked. She sat up and looked at Tuva quizzically.

"Our great lake. Our Lake Superior. Our great water or big sea," Tuva said, beaming.

"It is so magical," Franny said. "I have seen the ocean, of course, and this reminds me of it in some ways. But there is just something so different about this place."

"I couldn't agree more," Tuva said. "Yet another reason I believe you and I will get along great."

Franny started to laugh, but she quickly sobered. Tuva glanced around, wondering what caused her to frown. Adam was approaching with a somber look, carrying a small box in his hands. Tuva peeked over at Isak. A look of pain crossed his face before he shrugged his shoulders and smiled tenderly at Tuva.

Excusing herself with a mumble, Franny walked across the boat to stand next to Isak.

Tuva shifted in her seat preparing for a barrage as Adam sat down next to her. He cleared his throat and stared at the small box in his hands. There was nothing but the sound of water and the breeze between them. The silence drove Tuva's nerves over the edge.

"I don't know what to say," Adam finally said.

"Is that from Bill?" Tuva whispered.

"How did you know?" he asked, still not looking her way.

"Franny said something to me," she said.

"Bless her. She knew I was struggling with this," he said. "I wasn't sure what to say or if I should say anything at all."

"Did you say something to Isak about this?" Tuva asked.

"Not until this morning," Adam said, finally looking at her. "I think it still somewhat hurts and maybe confuses him, but this isn't about him. This is about my friend. And it is about you."

"Okay. As hard as this is, let's get this over," Tuva said.

"Before we went into battle at Gettysburg, he showed me this box and made me swear to give it to you if he didn't make it. It's almost like he knew,"

Adam said. He paused as though he was trying to figure out what to say next.

"If this is too difficult for you, we can wait," Tuva said. "Or just hand me the box."

"No," Adam said. "I made a promise." Then, clearing his throat, he continued by saying, "Before each battle, we always told each other to give our things to our loved ones, but until Gettysburg, he had never mentioned the box. A few times he would say, tell Tuva I loved her if I don't make it. So, this time, when he made me swear I would do this, I couldn't tell him no."

"Adam, I'm so sorry that you are now a part of this story," Tuva said.

"Don't be, Tuva," Adam said. "I learned what love was by watching this whole thing. The night before we went into battle, he told me that he knew you loved Isak. But his heart would always belong to you. He said he would die a happy man knowing that you received this box, that his last message to you would be given to you. His message is mostly written in a letter, but he also wanted me to tell you that he never regretted loving you. He hoped one day the memories you shared would be happy memories and not ones shrouded in sadness and heartache."

Tuva stared at Adam, not knowing what to say. Adam studied her in return before handing her the box. He mumbled something about leaving her to it and walked over to help Isak. Tuva looked over at her husband, but this time he didn't smile at her tenderly. He looked out toward the water, mumbled something to Adam, and then went below deck.

Wanting to go after her husband, she stood and started to follow, but Adam stopped her by saying, "He is trying to be respectful of you, Tuva. Let him give this to you."

Tuva looked over at Franny who had a look of compassion on her face and when she nodded her head as though to say, go ahead, Tuva sat back down. She stared at the box in front of her. She fumbled at the lid before opening it slowly. A gasp escaped her lips as she lifted a small portrait of herself. It had been drawn by pencil capturing her likeness so well it was like looking in a mirror.

Tuva studied it closely until she noticed Bill's initials in the corner. He had done this. He had drawn her face with her hair billowing around her as though it were blowing in the wind.

Instead of feeling sad, Tuva grew angry at this man for still finding a way to sneak into her life. She dropped the sketch and slammed the box shut. She threw it down and ran below.

As she ran past Isak, she whispered, "I need some space. Please give me a moment."

Isak obeyed her wishes and went up top. It took a while for Tuva to regain her composure. But once she collected herself, she went back on deck. The box was nowhere to be found. She was thankful it had disappeared, for she wasn't ready to face it yet. She waited for an onslaught of questions that never came and was even more thankful for her family.

Tuva went to stand by the railing and just watched the water.

Franny joined her shortly after and said, "It's such a gorgeous day. Don't you agree?"

Reaching over to grab Franny's hand, Tuva said, "It is indeed, sister. It is indeed."

"I like the sound of that. Sister."

"I do too."

"My only other sibling passed in the war, so having a sister and brothers now does my heart good," Franny said. "They, of course, do not take his place. But it is nice to belong again."

"Do you not have any other family?" Tuva asked.

"My only other family was our mother," Franny said, "but after my brother died, she gave up on life."

"I see," Tuva said. "I'm sorry for that."

"She and I were never close. But even still, losing her was heartbreaking," Franny said.

"Of course it was," Tuva said. "We will help you create your new home in our bay."

"That is something I have longed for, for some time," Franny said.

"I can't wait to show it to you," Tuva said. "You thought Duluth showed the magic of the lake. Just wait until we get to our bay."

"Adam talked so much about it that I have been counting down the days until we could be here."

Tuva smiled, and they looked out at the water. Feeling content to sit in silence, Tuva was hesitant to break it but was compelled to say, "Thank you for not asking."

"Tuva, I can't imagine how difficult this is for you," Franny said. "Adam didn't share all of it with me, but he did share more last night. He said everything else was only your story and not his. But I have heard enough to know you are so strong to endure all that you have and still be such a bright light for all that come near you."

A comfortable silence settled between them again, and the subject wasn't brought up for the rest of the journey. Adam pretended the conversation never took place, and Isak kept his distance. Tuva knew he kept away from her because she asked for it below, but she hoped he would figure out she needed it for just that moment, and not forever.

She grew weary of this dance between the three of them and made up her mind to face the box and then bury it and this triangular mess once and for all.

Chapter Forty-Five

Stirring the vegetables was a nice distraction for Tuva, even though she could tell Marriam was watching her closely. It was agreed upon they would have a giant feast to celebrate Adam's homecoming and his new bride, and Tuva dove into the preparations.

Marriam placed her hand on Tuva's and said, "I think the vegetables are well mixed, my daughter."

Tuva jerked and said, "Goodness, I'm a jumpy mess these days. So much excitement."

"Is that really all?" Marriam asked.

"I don't know what you mean," Tuva said.

"Okay, if you don't want to talk about it, that's fine, but when you're ready, I'm here," Marriam said.

"Too many around right now," Tuva whispered.

"I will need some help tomorrow. Perhaps you should come by in the morning," Marriam said.

"I would be happy to help."

"Good, now let's focus on our celebration," Marriam said.

"Yes, let's focus on that," Tuva said and forced a smile. She kept that expression plastered in place the rest of the evening and when everyone left, she finally let it fade before going to bed. She noticed Isak tried to reach out to her, but she was too tired and drifted into sleep, before having to get into a conversation she wasn't ready for.

The following morning dawned early, and Tuva rose before the sun. She wrapped her shawl around her shoulders and went out to welcome the morning by the shoreline. She breathed in the misty air and lifted her arms to the sky as the sun peaked in the distance. A noise sounded behind her, and she turned to see Isak standing a few feet back. He was looking toward the water, but she knew he was watching her closely.

The corners of her mouth lifted slightly, but her attempt at being jovial faltered at his expression. She looked back out toward the rising sun and tried to calm her racing thoughts.

"I don't know what to say or do," Isak said. "I just refuse to let this thing, this man, come between us again."

"I don't know what to say either," she said. "I thought this was resolved so long ago."

"But how could it be resolved when you never allowed yourself to examine how things were?"

"I don't know what you could possibly mean by that," Tuva said.

"That you have always loved him but won't ever admit it to me, because you don't want to face it or you don't want to hurt me," Isak said.

"Is that really what you believe?" she asked. "Isak, I love you. I have always loved you. I have always ever been in love with only you," Tuva said, walking toward her husband. "One day a man attacked me, tried to rape me, beat me. I still have scars on me from the gashes he created. And I still have bruises on my heart and soul from what he did." Tuva wrapped her arms around herself. "I felt broken and unholy and empty and ugly. And another man helped me not feel so much of those things. He treated me like I wasn't broken while your parents, God love them, did. I needed someone to make me feel like I was normal when I didn't feel normal, and he did that. And for that, he has a special place in my heart. But again, it isn't the same. It could never be the same." She grabbed Isak's hand. "I gave my heart and soul to you long before this happened. And they will always belong to you. Always. And it pains me that we are having to talk about this again."

"It makes me angry," Isak whispered.

"How do you think I feel?" Tuva said, dropping her hand and taking a step back. "On the boat, it wasn't sadness that caused me to need a minute. It was anger. I'm so angry at him, and at that man who attacked me that set these things in motion."

"I think I need some time to think about this."

"Isak, please tell me that I'm not about to lose you, lose us."

Isak shortened the distance between them and hugged her close. "No, it isn't that. I've just been looking at this all wrong. I didn't think to consider what things were really like for you. All this time, I was ignoring the biggest piece of this. Your attack. I just need some time to think about this and process it. I love you, my Tuva."

Kissing the top of her head, Isak let her go and walked back up to the cabin. Tuva watched him leave, but didn't follow. She wanted to give him the space he needed. She waited until he reemerged, dressed for the day. He waved at her and left in the direction of his workshop.

Tuva went to the cabin and threw herself into preparing for the day. She couldn't go see Marriam fast enough. She ignored the rumbling in her belly as she set out toward her mother-in-law's, but she didn't get far before Marriam was walking toward her with a basket in hand.

"Oh, did I misunderstand?" Tuva asked.

"No," Marriam said with a smile. "I just thought with a house full, it might be better for me to come to you."

"But I thought I was helping you with something this morning," Tuva said.

"I was going to have you help me make a pie while we chatted, but Isak stopped in to see me this morning, and I knew it would be best if I came to you."

Neither spoke the rest of the way to the cabin until they were both settled at the table with shortbread and coffee. Tuva fiddled with bites of biscuit until Marriam bent down to the basket next to her and pulled out the box from Bill.

She set it in front of Tuva. "You ready to do this?"

Tuva felt her eyes widen as she looked from Marriam to the box, and back to Marriam. "How did you get that?"

"Adam gave it to Isak and Isak gave it to me," Marriam said. "Isak told me he couldn't handle this, but knew it was important that this whole thing had the final closure it needed. Once and for all. But then this morning when he came to me, he said he was wrong about so many things. He told me that all he could ever focus on was seeing the two of you together that day on the dock. He thought he had to learn to forgive you for that, and he did. But in that, he realized he had forgotten your attack. He had never allowed himself to see that part of the story. He is angry at himself for that. He is angry for not being there for you and he is angry at the man that stole so much from you both."

"Bill?" Tuva asked.

"No, my daughter, the attacker," Marriam said gently.

"Marriam, what if I did love him?" Tuva asked.

"Oh, Tuva," Marriam said, reaching across the table to squeeze her hand. "Of course you loved him. We all loved him. He helped you put your pieces back together."

Tuva moved her mug and plate aside and placed the box in front of her. It was the first time she really studied it and realized it was an old cigar box. It was one that she had seen on his mantel often while they lived in his home in Duluth.

A lump formed in the back of her throat. She inhaled slowly, and asked, "Can you give me a minute?"

"I will be just outside," Marriam said. "Call for me when you are ready."

Tuva waited until Marriam shut the door behind her, then lifted the lid off the box. She picked up the drawing of her and stared at it. She noticed a fierce look in her eyes and realized this was how Bill had chosen to always see her despite the broken mess she was when he first met her.

Placing the picture next to the box, Tuva picked up a few more items. She stared at the picture of Bill in his uniform, and her heart skipped a beat. He did look handsome, but he looked almost sad. Like he had lost something precious to him and she wondered if he had been thinking of her. There was a little bit of money and an old watch, and she wondered about it, since she had never noticed it on him before.

She picked up a small booklet of poems he often carried in his pocket when he came to visit her. It had a marker in it, so she opened the book to that page. It was the poem of strength and beauty he had often quoted to her when she was struggling the most during her time of healing.

At the bottom of the box was a letter addressed to her. She fumbled with the paper as she opened it. Her mouth went dry, so she took a sip of her coffee. She breathed deep and began to read.

Tuva,

If you are reading this, then it means I'm gone, and I never had the chance to really tell you my heart. Yes, I shared pieces of it, but things were so complicated. I wish I could tell you that I'm sorry for falling in love with you. But loving you was one of the highest honors of my life, even though you did not love me the same. I know that your heart always belonged to another, and it always will. But I also know this—that I made a difference in your life when you needed that the most, and I have made peace with that being enough.

I will never forget the day I first saw you. You were standing there trembling. Your dress was ripped to shreds, and you were clinging to its fabric to cover yourself as much as you could. When I stepped closer to put my coat around you, I saw your face the first time. Your eyes were already swelling and turning colors. Your lower lip was bleeding and swollen. You had bruises and scratches on your face. You had a bleeding gash on your leg. There were scratches and bruises on your arms. But what will forever stay with me is the spark of defiance behind the sorrow in your eyes. And I knew I would never be the same. I knew I would do whatever I could from that day on to make sure you were okay and being taken care of and loved the way you deserved to be loved. I knew I was lost in love with you.

And then I discovered who you were. I tried to stay away, but every day I found myself at your doorstep making sure you were okay. I was drawn to you like I had never been drawn to another. I could see and feel your pain. It was never fair of me to put you in such a compromising situation, especially since your husband is my dearest friend and so much like a brother. It is funny, and yet a little tragic how much I love you both.

I want to share that the picture you are holding that I drew of you was one that I drew several weeks after your attack. It was after one of your rough days and you were desperately trying to hold it together. But even though you were struggling, you had this determination and strength in you that was so admirable. I had to capture you like that. It is that strength that I admire and love most about you.

I will end this letter with just a few short phrases from our favorite poem.

Your strength in the night that holds your head high.

Your beauty that comes from your heart.
May they both carry you home.
May they both carry you high.

I'm forever yours,

Bill

Tuva placed the letter on the table. Her heart pounded as the weight of what he wrote settled around her. She placed everything back into the box and called for Marriam.

When Marriam walked back into the cabin, Tuva wondered what she must look like, given the alarm on Marriam's face.

"You are visibly shaking, Tuva," Marriam said. "Are you okay?"

"I'm completely wrecked right now," Tuva said. "Please look at everything and tell me what I'm supposed to do."

Marriam gently thumbed through the contents. She studied the drawing of Tuva and whispered, "This is a beautiful portrait of you."

"He drew it soon after my attack," Tuva said.

"How do you know?" Marriam asked.

"It, um, is in the letter," Tuva stammered. "Please, read it."

Marriam unfolded the letter and began to read. When she was done, she placed it back in the box. "Isak needs to see this."

"You can't be serious."

"I have never been more serious," Marriam said. "The two of you have danced around this invisible triangle for far too long. You keep moving past it, but then it catches up to you. He needs to see that this wasn't born out of lust or anything against him. He needs to see it for what it was."

"Which is what?"

"A man fell in love with you. You didn't fall in love with him. You loved him like you love me and your brothers. You loved him for helping you heal. But you were never in love with him. You were close because of a shared experience resulted from a tragedy."

"How do I explain that to Isak?" Tuva asked.

"He will see it after he sees all of this," Marriam said.

"Are you sure?" Tuva asked.

"Tuva, you know your husband as well as I do."

"He will, won't he," Tuva said, trying to reassure herself.

"Have him read the letter first, then show him the rest of it," Marriam said.

"Okay," Tuva said. "I think I'm going to go for a walk, get some air. And then when he comes home for lunch, I will talk to him."

But Isak didn't go home for lunch. Tuva sat on the porch waiting for him and when he didn't come, she went for another walk. She steered clear of his workshop because she wanted to honor that he needed space. Tuva started to walk toward home when she happened upon her mother.

"Oh, there you are," her mother said.

"Mamma," Tuva said. "It still surprises me to see you here sometimes."

"Good surprise, I hope."

"Of course," Tuva said. "It was just so long that we were separated."

"I know. It's still a jolt for me too to run into you," her mother said. "But I was looking for you this time."

"Can I help with something?" Tuva asked.

"Tuva, I know what happened," she blurted out. "And before you get mad at Marriam, I made her tell me. Mamma to Mamma."

The ground seemed to move under Tuva's feet, and she had to steady herself.

Her mother rushed to her side and put her arm around her daughter. "Come have some coffee and biscuits with me. Let's talk of joyous things so that your heart will be ready for when your husband finds his way home."

Leaning against her mother, Tuva allowed herself to be led to Marriam's home. When she opened the front door, she found all the women of her community gathered with coffee and biscuits, waiting for her. Something inside her shifted, a weight lifted off her shoulders, and she let the rush of belonging soak into her soul.

Making her way to the chair offered to her, Tuva sat down and sipped the cup of coffee thrust into her hands. There was laughter and chatting from all around the table until Marriam clanged the side of her coffee cup and the room fell silent.

"Ladies, welcome to the first ever weekly coffee and biscuits," Marriam began. "My first daughter-in-law had this idea a long while ago, and after discussing it with Elin, we decided now was the perfect time to gather."

"Oh, my goodness, you remembered," Tuva said.

Marriam beamed at Tuva. "My daughter, you are facing a great hardship. One of many you have faced over the years. You have met each one with a strength and determination that is envied by so many. And you have often faced those hardships alone. But you are not alone today. Lean on us, your sisters, your mammas, your neighbors, your community. The community that you have been building. None of us would be here today if it wasn't for you bringing us together."

"To our strong and fearless leader of the bay, Tuva," her mother said, raising her coffee cup in the air.

"To Tuva," everyone else said in unison.

The hum of voices and merriment picked up again, while Tuva looked across the table at her two mothers and mouthed, "Thank you."

Both women raised their cups as if to say, you're welcome, then clinked their cups together and joined the chatter.

Chapter Forty-Six

Tuva brushed her hand over the space next to her in bed and found the spot warm but empty. She sat up just as the door to the cabin shut. Isak had left again before she had woken up, and she was growing frustrated.

It had been a week since Marriam had given her the box and she wasn't sure why Isak was avoiding her so much. He would leave early and come home late. He was never disrespectful or mean, but would say little before telling Tuva he loved her and would go to bed.

But that morning, Tuva'd had enough. She flew the covers back and quickly got dressed. She rushed to tidy the bed and make coffee. She needed as much gumption this morning as she could muster, because today was the day they were going to face this and move on.

She had planned this moment all week, but since Isak wasn't having any of it at home, Tuva decided to take the box to him at his workshop. Tuva ate a small breakfast and drank her coffee, trying to prepare in her mind what she would do or say. When she was ready, she threw on her coat, wrapped her shawl around her arms, grabbed the box, and stomped out the door.

It didn't take long to walk to her husband's workshop. She stood outside the door, took in a deep breath, let it out slowly, and flung the door open with a loud bang. All commotion halted at the sound and all eyes were on her.

Tuva sauntered into the workshop, shoved the box onto a table in front of her, and yelled, "Everyone needs to leave! Now. I need to have a word with my husband."

The men exchanged glances and quickly left out the same door Tuva had shoved open. When Adam was leaving, he gave her a wink before closing the door behind him. Tuva looked back over at Isak, and she could tell he was trying to stifle a grin, but he didn't move toward her and didn't say a word.

"Since you won't do this at home. I have no choice but to bring it to you here," she said.

"Bring what to me here?" Isak asked.

"Our mess. This box. Our words. Our whatever you want to call it."

Isak started to walk toward Tuva slowly, and it took everything within her not to run into his arms.

When he stopped inches from her, she took a step back, snatched the box, and thrust it between them.

"We must face this. And you need to see this."

"I don't think I can," he whispered.

"What is it that we keep saying to each other? That we need to face things together," Tuva said. "It doesn't feel like we are doing that right now. And I need you now more than ever."

"Why?" Isak whispered.

"Because my heart is breaking without you. Because I'm scared of losing another child. Because I worry about Wally. Because I lost a dear friend, and so did you, and we are grieving apart instead of together."

"What do you want me to say?" he asked.

"Nothing, yet," Tuva said as she lifted the lid off the box and handed him the letter from Bill. "You need to read this."

"I can't," Isak said.

"I didn't think I could either," Tuva said. "But I need for you to do this."

Isak grabbed the letter and took a step back. He unfolded it without taking his eyes off Tuva.

"Please, my Isak."

Isak's face softened, and he looked down at the paper and started to read. Tuva watched him warily, and she could tell when he got to the part about her attack.

His face paled, he gasped, covered his mouth, stumbled back and sat on a stool, but he kept reading.

Tuva knew the second he was done, even though he didn't move. She was caught in a trance as the letter flitted to the ground in front of Isak. He didn't look up at her, and she couldn't move. She was sure her heart was going to pound out of her chest before Isak finally lifted his head to meet her gaze. But he still said nothing.

Tuva finally whispered, "Please, Isak, say something."

"Tuva, please. I'm trying to figure out how to say this."

"Okay. Take your time."

Isak stood up from his stool. "Please don't say anything until I'm finished. This isn't easy for me."

"I promise."

"I will never forget the first time I saw you," Isak began. "You were walking along the road with your sister and a wagon came rumbling by going too fast and it almost knocked your sister over. You jumped into the road and although I couldn't hear what you said, I could see the look of fire on your face. And I knew then I had to meet you."

"I never knew that," Tuva said.

"Please, my Tuva,"

"Sorry."

"I know why Bill fell in love with you. It is the same reason I fell in love with you. And I can't fault him for that. Especially under the circumstances. And oh my god, Tuva."

A look of panic flashed across Isak's face as realization seemed to set in, and he rushed to her. He lifted her leg, gently raised her skirt, and tugged at her stockings, before his thumb caressed the jagged scar from her attack.

"I didn't realize it was so bad," Isak continued. "I mean, I should have because of the way you explained it. But I didn't let myself see how bad it was for you. I couldn't let my mind go there. I was so hurt when I found you two together, and I had already conjured in my mind what it must have been like between you. I was so wrong about it. I have never been so wrong about anything in my life."

"Isak," Tuva whispered.

"How did you get the gash on your leg, and so high up?" Isak asked gently.

"The man was chasing me, and I fell on a sharp stick. When he lunged on top of me again, he ripped my clothes apart as I tried to get free. The more I thrashed, the more violent he became. At one point I felt the jagged edge of the stick rip against my flesh, then he bore down on me again and I couldn't move my leg away from its sharp edge. I honestly didn't realize it was so bad until a few days later. It was struggling to heal, so I had Marriam examine it and we realized it needed more than a bandage. So, Marriam stitched it for me."

Tears trickled down Isak's cheek as he studied Tuva. She reached out and wiped the moisture away. "It's okay, my Isak. I'm okay. It no longer hurts like it once did."

"And Bill helped with that," Isak mumbled.

"Yes, he did," Tuva said. "Any person who would have showed me such care would have."

"I know," Isak whispered. "I keep seeing you, as Bill described you in his letter. It's such a vivid description. I'm so sorry."

"Please don't feel sorry for me."

Isak threw open the lid of the box, rummaged around, pulled out the picture of Tuva and held it up. "This woman is not one who needs anyone to feel sorry for her. This is the same woman I fell in love with. And this is the same woman that came marching in here today demanding her husband stop being such a coward and face what she had to face alone all these years. No, I do not feel sorry for her. I'm more in love with her today than ever before. I admire her more than ever. And I couldn't want her more than I do right at this moment."

Charging into her husband's arms, Tuva kissed him passionately. When she pulled away from him, they were both out of breath, and he stumbled back. "Christ, woman. I may just take you here in the shop."

"What's stopping you?"

Tuva felt radiant, knowing she was the cause of desire flaring in her husband's eyes as he moved closer to her.

"If you insist, my Tuva."

Chapter Forty-Seven

Shutting the lid, Tuva placed the box on the table in between her and Isak. She took a sip of her water. She tried to take another bite of food, but Tuva found she was no longer hungry, and was just messing with her water and plate to help distract her.

"Is this everything?" Isak asked.

"Yes," Tuva said. "He didn't want me to have much. Just these few things."

"What do you want to do with it?" Isak asked.

"I have thought long and hard about it," Tuva said. "I think I want to bury the box in our family plot and have a memorial service for him."

"I like that idea, but I want the picture he drew of you," Isak said. "I'm sure that sounds morbid, but he drew you so well. And I love the look of defiance he captured in your eyes. I want to keep it."

Surprised, Tuva reached into the box and pulled out the picture. She handed it to her husband. "It's yours."

"I think you should keep the picture of Bill and the booklet of poems," Isak said.

"Wouldn't that be weird for you?"

"No weirder than this whole situation."

"I will bury his letter along with the rest of the contents inside the box. And just so there are no secrets between us, I want you to know that I plan to write him a letter of response to bury with it. If you want to read it, you can," Tuva said.

"No, I don't need to," Isak said, as he stared at the picture of Tuva. "I have to tell you. I tried to look at the box one time without you."

"When did you do that?"

"Right before I gave it to Mamma," Isak said. "I was so angry, and I wanted to find proof that you were lying to me. But then I opened the box and saw the picture of you laying on top. I was so caught off guard, and then I was afraid of the truth. I think I knew down deep that what I was telling myself was the lie, and I was the one that was wrong. But I just couldn't face it."

There was a knock at the door, and Isak went to answer. Adam walked in, glancing at Tuva.

She smiled brightly and asked, "Can I get you a plate, brother?"

"Haha, no. Thank you though," Adam said. "Franny fed me well. I came as soon as I could. Supplies landed about an hour ago and along with it came a letter. They think they found Wally but are not certain."

"What?" Tuva asked, standing.

"Is there more news than that?" Isak asked.

"Just that they think he was captured by the enemy after the battle. He was wounded, but is being taken care of. They thought he was being imprisoned at one location, but found that wasn't the case. But they at least believe he may be alive."

"This is great news," Isak said. "Did you tell Mamma and Pappa?"

"Not yet. I wanted us to go over there together. Franny is waiting outside."

"Why is she outside?" Tuva asked.

"Well, we weren't sure how things were going, so wanted to be respectful," Adam said.

"I appreciate your concern, but you are not overstepping or being disrespectful," Tuva said.

"So, your outburst at the workshop helped?" Adam asked with a smirk.

"I think you know the answer to that question," she said. "And who is being disrespectful now?"

"Just teasing, sis," Adam said.

Tuva put on her coat and grabbed her shawl, while Isak gathered the dishes and placed them in a neat pile by the wash basin.

"Wow, you have trained him well," Adam said.

"Watch it now," Isak said with a snort.

Tuva smiled at the comradery. It had been missing between them, and she was pleased it had returned. Things were finally going to be okay.

She followed Adam out the door, greeted Franny and said, "Next time, please come in. It is growing colder, and there is no sense in freezing just to save face."

"Sounds like a great plan to me," Franny said. "It's just I'm new here."

"Nonsense," Tuva said. "You are family. Don't forget that."

Franny giggled. "Okay, I will try not to."

Adam linked arms with Tuva, and asked, "Can I chat with you while we walk?"

Tuva glanced at Franny and noticed her wink at Adam, and her stomach lurched, knowing what was to come. Isak smacked his brother's back as though to encourage him, then led Franny along the path, to allow his brother and wife a chance to talk.

"I'm growing nervous. What is this about?" Tuva asked.

Adam cleared his throat. "So, you're okay then?"

"Yes. Adam, please don't fret."

"When I was in the hospital mending from my injuries. I stared at that box every day. I told myself it was not my place to ever look at its contents, but I worried that something might happen to it, so I looked inside," Adam said.

"You read the letter," Tuva said.

"I read the letter," he said. "It was none of my business and for that, I'm so sorry."

"Did you tell Franny about it?"

"I did end up telling her," Adam said. "You know the whole, 'don't keep secrets from your wife' philosophy that you and Isak keep spouting. Please don't be angry with me. I'm truly sorry."

"It's okay," she said. "It's easier somehow knowing that everyone knows that needs to know, so that no one looks at me questioning or wondering."

"Tuva," Adam started. Stopped. Tried again. "Tuva, I'm sorry for what happened to you. Bill painted a hard picture. I'm sorry you were hurt so viciously, sis."

A lump rose in her throat before she said, "Oh, Adam, it seems so long ago."

"So, you're okay now?" Adam asked.

"I will be honest. That attack will stay with me forever," she said, "but all that is left are scars. And you know how scars are. Sometimes they have a twinge of pain, but they become bearable."

"You are the strongest person I know," Adam said.

"Enough of sad things," Tuva said. "Let's focus on Wally now."

Tuva pushed the conversation with Adam aside for now, but she hated the thought that any of her family would look at her as though she were glass about to break.

Marriam threw the door of the cabin open, breaking into Tuva's thoughts. "Is it Wally?"

"We have some news, Mamma," Adam said.

"Is he gone?" Marriam asked.

"Not that we know," Isak said. "How about we go inside and discuss this?"

When everyone was settled, Marriam shot Tuva a look followed by a wink, before turning to listen to Adam. Once everything was explained, Tuva offered to help get some coffee on. Marriam indicated there was pie and biscuits if anyone wanted a sweet bite to eat, so Tuva said she would put them out as well.

Tuva was deep in thought, so didn't hear Franny approach until she asked if she could help with anything. Tuva spilled the coffee grounds on the counter and laughed at her blunder.

"Goodness, I'm sorry I startled you," Franny said.

"It's okay," Tuva said. "My nerves are a little frazzled these days."

"And why wouldn't they be," Franny said. "Memories, so many feelings, facing wounds of the past, Wally. It would make sense that you are frazzled."

"Thank you for understanding," Tuva said.

"But there is something you are not and that is weak," Franny said.

"What?" Tuva asked.

"I could tell by your expression when talking with Adam that you think we look at you as though you are weak," Franny said. "I don't think you're weak."

"I do wonder if that is how they all view me sometimes," Tuva said.

"How do we view you?" Marriam asked as she reached up to gather plates off the shelf next to Tuva.

"She thinks we look at her as weak," Franny said.

Marriam chuckled. "My dear, you are the least weak person in this room."

"And dare I say in the bay," Franny said.

Tuva's lips curled, and she gathered mugs to take to the table. "That makes me feel better. But I think Isak hasn't figured that out yet."

"He will," Marriam said. "He just realized you are a survivor of something horrific. Let's give him some time to process things."

The family gathered around pie and coffee while the conversation turned to the next big project on the bay—Adam and Franny's home. They wanted to build closer to the store and the docks. Adam indicated he wanted to focus on building up the docks, but in a separate area from where it was currently. Instead of straight into the bay, he wanted it off to the side, opposite Tuva and Isak's ridge.

Isak gave his blessing for his brother's plans, and Tuva offered to help Franny sew some curtains for their new home.

Everyone was in a happier mood as the conversation lulled, and Tuva said, "Perhaps it is time for Isak and I to head home."

"Yes, but first we have something to share," Isak said.

Marriam glanced at Tuva before asking, "Is it good news?"

"Tuva and I have decided to have a memorial service for Bill, here in our bay, as a family," Isak said.

Feeling the color leave her face, Tuva said, "We are going to bury his box with his things and have a small marker made. He will be buried in the family plot."

"Are you okay with this, Isak?" Josef asked.

"Yes, Pappa," Isak said. "This is what is best."

"We can discuss more of this later," Tuva said. "We have plenty of time to figure things out."

"When do you want to do this?" Marriam asked.

"I was thinking in the spring," Isak said.

"I think that is a lovely idea," Tuva said. "Right after the baby comes."

Adam raised his glass in the air and said, "To babies, to Bill, and to new beginnings."

"Here, here, son," Josef said.

"To new beginnings," Isak and Tuva said, with eyes on only each other.

Chapter Forty-Eight

Dear Wally,

I don't even know why I keep writing to you. Maybe it's because I hope that one day you will be found safe and will get these letters. Maybe it's more for me. Either way, if you get to read this, I hope it prepares you for when you come home, since so much has happened since you left.

Our bay keeps growing. A few more families have settled here. And Nora heard from some friends in Sweden who plan to come in a year or two. And they want to settle here too.

I think it's time we made this an official little community. Don't you?

I keep praying for your safe return.

Your ever devoted sis,

Tuva

P.S. You have a nephew. You won't believe what we named him. It was Isak's idea.

Chapter Forty-Nine

The bouquet of flowers fluttered in the breeze as Tuva laid it on the porch in front of her. She was happy with how it turned out. She decided to make a second one for anyone else who might want to put flowers on the fresh gravestone. The plans to have a memorial celebration for Bill had come together smoothly, but it was delayed into the summer due to difficulties in having her son.

A small sound from the basket next to her feet caused Tuva to pause. She placed the flowers next to the bouquet and bent down to pick up the small bundle.

"My sweet baby boy," Tuva crooned.

"You will never get anything accomplished if you pick him up every time he makes a sound," Marriam teased as she rounded the corner.

"What do you expect?" Tuva said. "He is our little miracle."

"I half expected Minwaadizi to make an appearance. With all the difficulty you had bringing him into the world," Marriam said.

"Wouldn't that have been a wondrous thing? I miss her so much," Tuva said, studying her infant. "Do you think he is hungry?"

"You just fed him," Isak said in a teasing tone, walking out of the cabin. "Hi, Mamma."

"Son," Marriam said, with a smile and a nod.

"How about you give him to Farmor, so you can keep working on your task," Marriam said, holding out her arms.

Tuva giggled. "I'm sure he would love to see his grandmother."

Marriam cradled the baby and walked to sit in the rocking chair. She hummed a Swedish lullaby Tuva hadn't heard since she was a child, and it made her grin widen. It faded quickly, though, as her thoughts turned to Wally. She wondered where he could be.

"Are you okay?" Isak asked.

"Yes, just thinking of our brother," Tuva whispered.

"I woke up thinking about him too," Isak said. "Adam said he sent out three more letters last week, but he said with how things are in the war, he doesn't anticipate hearing anything anytime soon."

"Isak, I had a thought," Tuva said, changing the subject. She could tell it was starting to upset Marriam.

"What grand scheme are you cooking up now?" Isak said.

"This is the grandest one yet," Tuva said.

"Let me guess," Isak said. "Should I dust off my suit so that I can be a proper mayor?"

"Don't make fun," Tuva said. "I think it's time. Several more families are wanting to build homes in our little bay. The expansion of the services we started offering in the spring has led to that. Just think about the legacy we could leave for our son and our grandchildren."

"We have so many projects right now. I can't imagine adding that to our plate," Isak said.

"Promise me that you will think on it," Tuva said. "The bank building is almost finished and with the store expanding along with the boarding house. Not to mention the fishing business gaining momentum. We have quite the little town forming."

"She has a point, Isak," Marriam said, not looking away from the baby.

"Let's get through the next couple of days, and I will think about it," Isak said.

Tuva thought about pushing the issue but decided against it, and went back to her chore of preparing the flowers for the memorial service. The service was going to be close family, but the rest of the community was going to come together for a late afternoon picnic. It would be held in an area Isak had cleared specifically for community gatherings. Several picnic tables were built and placed strategically, and Tuva couldn't think of a better way to remember a friend.

Tuva finished arranging the flowers and realized she barely had time to change and get ready for the little service. She gathered up her son, fed him, and prepared to head out with Isak to the family graveyard.

Before they left, Isak pulled Tuva into his arms and whispered, "I love you so much, my Tuva."

"And I you, my Isak."

The family walked to the little marker Adam had created for Bill. Isak carried the baby so Tuva could carry the flowers and box. Everyone else was already gathered around the small hole in the ground.

Isak winked at Tuva. "Thank you all for coming together. For supporting us in this process. For helping us mourn the loss of a friend. Bill was my brother. Bill was a helper to Tuva in a great time of need. And his memory will live forever in our hearts."

Tuva wiped at the moisture forming in her eyes and knelt to place the box into the ground. She pulled out a piece of paper, wrapped it around some of the flowers she'd prepared earlier, and laid it on the box.

She grabbed a handful of dirt. "Your strength in the night that holds your head high. Your beauty that comes from your heart. May they both carry you home. May they both carry you up high."

Sprinkling the dirt on the box, Tuva continued, "Goodbye, my dear friend. I love you, Bill." She kissed her hand, placed it on the marker, and went to stand next to Isak.

Isak studied Tuva as she reached for their son. Their fingers grazed as the baby was deposited into her arms and she warmed at his touch. She could tell Isak noticed her reaction to him, and he kissed her on the cheek.

"Adam, I believe, wanted to say something," Isak said.

Moving his way toward the front of the group, Adam started his little speech, but stopped when there was movement on the path behind the gathering. There were gasps, murmurs, and smiles and all eyes fell on Tuva, who was craning her neck to see what was going on.

"What is it?" Tuva asked, taking a few steps so she could see what was going on.

"It is only I, my friend."

Tuva recognized the voice instantly and stopped just as the group parted, allowing for Tuva to get a clearer picture.

"Minwaadizi," Tuva choked out.

Marriam reached for the baby so Tuva could rush to her friend's side. Tuva paused in front of Minwaadizi and her children and stared into her friend's troubled eyes before flinging her arms around her. Tuva let her tears rain down unchecked as she embraced her dearest friend.

"How is it that you always find your way to me when I need you the most?" Tuva asked.

"This time I come for selfish reasons," Minwaadizi said, "but I can explain that later. For now, let us remember our friend Bill."

Everyone gathered around Bill's grave once more, and Adam started his speech. Tuva let the tears flow when necessary and laughed when his words called for it. When he was done, Isak said a few more words before indicating it was time to gather for the picnic. Tuva wanted a few moments alone with the memory of Bill, so Isak ushered everyone along.

The family dispersed. Marriam took the baby and Minwaadizi's children with her. Isak and Minwaadizi hung back a few feet, and Tuva moved closer to the marker.

She knelt in front of it. "What a way for our paths to cross in life. My letter to you says it all, but I hope you know how much I appreciated our friendship. I was so lost and battered, and you were the shining light that helped me on my path to heal. Thank you for being there when I needed someone. Thank you for helping me put my pieces back together. Thank you for loving me. Rest in peace, my dear Bill."

Tuva picked up the shovel and started covering the little box and flowers. Minwaadizi, not saying a word, appeared at her side, and started to help. Tuva glanced around, realizing Isak had left to join the rest of the family.

"I told him to go," Minwaadizi said.

"Was he okay?" Tuva asked.

"Yes."

A comfortable silence fell over them as they finished their task. Tuva stacked the shovels against a tree and walked over to the only other marker in the family graveyard.

"You came to me that night," Tuva said. "You helped me say goodbye to my baby, Willow. And you have helped me now to say goodbye to my friend."

"I always find it interesting to see how things turn out in life," Minwaadizi said. "Your baby boy is beautiful, Tuva."

"Thank you. Your son and daughter have grown so much," Tuva said. She started to ask about Makwa, but read the look on her friend's face. "He is gone, isn't he?"

"Yes."

"I am so sorry, my friend. When did he die?"

"We lost him last summer," Minwaadizi said. "I tried to make it on my own, but found I needed to seek out the only family I had left."

"Welcome home, sister," Tuva said. "You will find your place here. As my friend, my sister, and as a member of this community. Come, let's join the others as we celebrate a life."

The women linked arms and joined the rest of the family. Tuva explained to Isak they would be having guests living with them for a time, and he welcomed Minwaadizi with open arms.

The rest of the community had already gathered and set up the food. As people were finishing their meal, Adam pulled out his fiddle and jumped right into a lively tune.

Tuva cheered him on. "It's been a long time since I heard you play."

"I figured the events that have occurred were cause for it," Adam said.

Isak pulled Tuva into a dance along with the others. The gaiety and music echoed across the bay. Tuva twirled around but told Isak she had to stop to catch her breath. He bowed to her playfully and gently pulled her away from the rest of the dancers.

When they were settled at a picnic table away from the others, she said she was going to rest a moment before rescuing her mother from having to watch the baby.

"I don't think it is such a hardship," Isak said, beaming at Tuva.

"Maybe, but I ..." Tuva trailed off and stood up.

"Is everything okay?" Isak asked.

"Everything is finally just perfect," Tuva said and took off running.

"Tuva, stop. Where are you going?" Isak asked, but followed her.

Tuva didn't stop. She knew running was probably not the best, given she was still recovering from giving birth to her baby several months ago, but she couldn't stop. It seemed like she would never make it to the water, but soon she was careening down the dock and headlong into her brother's arms.

"Wally!" Tuva screeched.

Wally laughed and swung Tuva around, hugging her tight. Isak was close behind and yelled out his brother's name before pulling them both into a hug. The three whooped, cried, and repeated each other's names, reminding Tuva of her reunion with Nora.

"It is such a wondrous day for you to be here," Tuva said. "But how are you here? The last we heard, you were still not found."

"A war tends to slow down communication," Wally said.

Tuva studied Wally. She could tell he had his own demons to conquer, but the same light, with a hint of mischief, still sparkled in his eyes, and she was thankful for it.

"I can't wait to hear your story, but for now, you must come and see the rest of the family."

"You said you were building a town, Tuva, but I didn't realize how much you had already accomplished," Wally said. "I hardly recognized the bay."

"I'm sure it is hard to believe all that has changed since you left," Tuva said, linking her arm with his. Isak gave instructions to the crewman on where to deposit Wally's things before following behind.

"So, my big brother is a big leader now. And I hear a father," Wally said over his shoulder.

Isak chuckled and asked, "What has my wife been telling you in her letters?"

"You did receive my letters, then?" Tuva asked.

"I received some of them once I was released and being checked out at the army hospital, but I'm sure some were lost," Wally said. "What is this celebration you are having?"

"It is a memorial and celebration of life for Bill," Isak said.

Wally halted and turned to look down at Tuva. "Did you receive what he wanted to give you?"

"I did," Tuva said. "Adam took care of that."

"Adam is here?" Wally asked, looking around.

"You didn't know?" Tuva asked.

"No, I got only a few of the letters that talked mostly of the bay and you and Isak," Wally said. "I heard Adam was hurt. I received some basic medical treatment, was discharged, and I came home. I asked around, but they said they thought he got married to a local girl, but I couldn't find out anything after that."

"He did get married. But he brought her home to us," Tuva said.

Wally asked more questions as they walked back toward the party. Tuva was surprised no one else seemed to notice they were gone. But the music and dancing were lively, so assumed everyone was distracted. Well, almost everyone. Minwaadizi waved at Tuva when they walked back into the circle.

Adam was in the middle of a new song when he glanced toward Tuva and screeched his violin to a halt. "Wally!"

Tuva and Isak stood back as the rest of the Nilsson family welcomed Wally home. Marriam was sobbing and hugging her youngest child while Josef couldn't seem to stop saying his name and clapping him on the back. Adam kept saying he was sorry that he lost sight of him on that day, and Franny grinned from ear to ear, taking it all in.

Nora walked over to Tuva and handed her the baby. "I can't deal with this day, Tuva. Sadness, reunions. So many emotions. Tobias is going to take our three to rest. That way I can help Marcy and Mamma with tidying up out here. You Nilssons need to go spend some time together. And we will bring you some refreshments later."

Tuva hugged her sister and thanked her before joining the fray. Wally realized the baby boy was present just as a hush fell on the Nilsson family circle.

"And who do we have here?" Wally asked.

Tuva grinned. "Wally, meet your nephew. Wilhelm Walter."

Beaming, Isak said, "We are calling him Billy."

Chapter Fifty

The sun sparkled across the water as Tuva walked along the bank. She had the latest newspaper in her hand, and she couldn't wait to show it to Isak. Hammers pounding in nails echoed across the water, and she skipped a little as excitement flooded through her. It had been several months since the war ended, and as she predicted, they had more people coming to their little bay wanting to settle there.

Minwaadizi fell into step beside her as Tuva neared the trail leading up to her home on the point.

"You are beaming," Minwaadizi said. "Is there another bundle that we should be preparing for?"

"No, nothing like that," Tuva said. "I'm beginning to think that perhaps I'm not meant for a lot of children, since I'm so busy with Isak building our legacy."

"Do you remember our first conversation here?" Minwaadizi asked. "I remember your eyes were wide with wonderment at how desolate it was, but you had this determination to see it through. Whatever it would be."

"I do," Tuva said, chuckling. "Now look at it."

"You have cared for this land well. Honored it in a way that would have brought Makwa joy, I think," Minwaadizi said.

"It has been a while since you have spoken of him," Tuva said.

"My heart is filling with love for another," Minwaadizi said.

"I suspected as much," Tuva said. "And what a match. Two of my favorite people, coming together. I can't wait for the day I can officially welcome you as a part of the Nilsson family."

"Now that we have talked about why I'm glowing, what is bringing the bounce in your step?" Minwaadizi asked.

Tuva handed the newspaper to Minwaadizi. "This."

Minwaadizi read where Tuva pointed. "I understand now."

Laughing outright, Tuva folded the paper and linked arms with her friend. She chatted about other things the rest of the way, but halted when she rounded the front of the cabin. Marriam was clapping and cheering while little Billy was struggling to take his first steps.

Tuva rushed to Marriam's side to help cheer her little boy on. Billy's face lit up when he saw his mamma. He started to clap his hands together before taking a few short steps and throwing himself at Tuva.

Giggling, Tuva swung her baby boy around and applauded his efforts. Minwaadizi's son tugged on Tuva's skirts and asked to take Billy back so they could go play together on the blanket. Tuva handed him over and a faint memory flitted through her mind.

She glanced over at her friend and asked," Do you remember what you told me?"

"That one day our children would play together," Minwaadizi said. "I think of that often."

Isak walked out of the cabin, and Tuva beamed at her husband saying, "I have something to show you."

"I can't wait to see it since you are so giddy about it," Isak said. "Especially since our son just walked his first steps, and yet you are still distracted."

"I am so happy you saw him," Tuva said.

"I did, but didn't want to startle him, so I watched from the window," Isak said. "Now what is this that you want to show me?"

Tuva unfolded the newspaper and read, "If given the chance, one must take a small boat ride or ride the trail to check out the lake's newest community. Founders Isak and Tuva Nilsson have created a place for people to start anew, surrounded by those who have a strong sense of community, are open to all, and have love for family. But be careful, once you step foot in this peaceful place, you may decide you will want to make it your home, too."

"Let me see that," Isak said, snatching the paper playfully out of Tuva's hands.

"It goes on to list the different businesses we have created. The number of families who live here and it even describes the most beautiful garden created by me," Tuva said.

Isak finished reading, folded the paper, and hugged Tuva. "Look what you have done, my Tuva."

"Look what we have done, my Isak," Tuva said. "It's amazing what we are accomplishing since we are, in fact, in it together."

"I remember those words," Isak said before kissing his wife.

"Goodness, the heat radiating off you two is scorching," Marriam said.

"Mamma," Isak admonished playfully, but didn't bother to look her way.

"Seriously, every time I walk up here, they are all over each other," Wally said, coming around the corner and stopping beside Minwaadizi.

Tuva didn't miss the look exchanged between her friend and her brother and she couldn't stop herself from saying, "Talk about heat."

Wally's face turned scarlet while Tuva howled. Minwaadizi linked her arm with Wally's, pulling his face down to hers for a kiss.

Marriam giggled. "Perhaps I should take the children somewhere else."

Wally lifted his head. "No, actually, we can't stay. Isak and Tuva, you are wanted down at the docks."

"Mamma, do you mind watching Billy a little longer?" Tuva asked.

"I prefer to call it spending time with my grandchild," Marriam said. Then to Minwaadizi, she said, "You can go with them too if you want. This way, I can spend time with all my grandchildren."

Tuva and Isak led the way to the docks where Tuva noticed a second boat had landed since she had walked home earlier. She must have been lost in her excitement to have missed it. As they neared the edge of the little marina, Tuva instantly recognized the man walking toward them.

"Joshua," Isak said, extending his hand. "What a pleasure it is to see you again."

"I read this delightful article in the newspaper and had to come check things out for myself," Joshua said. "Plus, I heard you were preparing some sort of celebration and thought it would be fun to be here for it."

Tuva hugged Joshua. "We are delighted you could make it."

"While you are here, you should visit Bill's grave. I can show you later if you want," Isak said.

"Dear Bill. I heard you have your own little Billy now," Joshua said. "Strange how things turn out."

"It is indeed," Tuva said. A gentle breeze rustled some leaves, causing them to fly in between them, and Bill's presence settled around her. By the expression on Isak's face, Tuva knew he felt it too. A look of love and understanding passed between them.

"So, what is this celebration you are planning?" Joshua asked.

"Nothing original, just a Founder's Day celebration," Isak said.

"It may not be original, but it's still exciting to build such a thing, Isak," Joshua said.

"Oh, I can't take the credit for this. This was all made possible by the support and ideas of my Tuva," Isak said.

"I can't wait to see it," Joshua said.

Isak nodded at Tuva, and her face broke into a wide grin. She spread her arms as though to encompass the whole cove.

"Welcome to Willow Bay!"

Acknowledgements

I want to thank all my family and friends who have supported me on my second book. I especially can't forget to mention the love and support from my daughter, Bri, and my three littles. You continue to cheer me on and recognize that when mom is working, she needs to have her time to focus. Your honor, love, and respect through this process always encourages me to keep going.

I would like to thank the Chisago County Historical Society for giving me access to the resources you have. The curators of the museum and historical society answered my questions and helped point me in the right direction when furthering my research for this book.

I especially want to thank my dear friends, the YaYas. You all have supported me, cheered me on, and held space for me when I needed it. I also must mention my amazing friends in WomenLead. Your encouragement helped spur me on when I doubted myself.

Thank you to my proofreaders who jumped at the chance to help. And a special thank you to Melanie Cooper who has been with me every step of this book providing sound advice, being an ear when I need it, and reassuring me through it all.

And finally, I can't forget to honor and thank the help I have received from my editor, Jeanne Felfe. Thank you for your continued faith in me and your immeasurable feedback and wisdom.

A Note to Readers

Thank you for reading *Great Water, Big Sea*.

If you enjoyed it, I would appreciate a review on your favorite retailer website.

And I'd love to hear from you. Drop me a line at esther@theestherschultz.com

My website is theestherschultz.com

About The Author

Esther Schultz lives by her personal motto of, "be kind always and spread joy every day." She believes everyone can live a peaceful, joy-filled life and attempts to spread that message in her work and daily life. Her favorite things include spending time in nature, especially along Lake Superior, and advocating for mental health. Esther lives in central Minnesota with her husband, four children, her dog, and horse.

Made in the USA
Monee, IL
23 October 2023

45073645R00225